I0544139

DISCOVERED BETRAYAL

DISCOVERED BETRAYAL

THE DISCOVERED TRUTH SERIES ROMANTIC SUSPENSE
BOOK FIVE

JULIE BAWDEN DAVIS

Roses
ARE
RED
PUBLISHING

Copyright © 2020 Roses are Red Publishing

All rights reserved.

Cover by Judy Bullard (customebookcovers.com)

Book design by Jeremy Davis

Palm logo design by Kayla Curry

Roses are Red logo design by Kyle Kane

No part of this book may be reproduced, scanned, or distributed in any printed or electronic form without written permission from the publisher—Roses Are Red (www.RosesAreRedpublishing.com). Please don't participate in or encourage piracy of copyrighted materials in violation of the author's rights. Thank you for respecting the hard work of this author.

This is a work of fiction. Characters and incidents are the product of the author's imagination. Any perceived likenesses are coincidental.

ISBN-13: 978-1-7345012-3-0

ISBN-10: 1-7345012-3-5

Distributed by Roses Are Red Publishing

rosesareredpublishing.com

❀ Created with Vellum

To all who have lost one another and found their way home to one another once again.

Tony Molinaro slid into a booth in a dark corner of the bar and glanced around. No one appeared to be casing the place for him. Good.

A waitress approached. "Can I get you anything, honey?"

Yeah, a bulletproof vest, he thought, but he smiled instead and said, "Sure, sugar, how about a plate of your tacos? And a beer. Stella will do."

She leaned her weight on one hip. "You been here before? I haven't seen you."

"It's been awhile."

"Well, welcome back to San Diego," she said, sidling off to place his order.

He appreciatively watched her wiggle away. But he had bigger things to think about right now. Like how Operation Ottoman went sideways without warning.

Except for missing Joanna, things had been good in Mexico. Low key. That is, until three days ago, when they stormed his home in Puerto Vallarta, and he had barely escaped. Now he had nowhere to go. Literally. He was getting too old for this shit.

When a busboy came back and set his beer on the table, Tony grabbed it and took a long pull. Ice cold. He'd had a hell of a time keeping his brews chilled enough in the Puerto Vallarta jungle with the solar-powered system he had rigged up.

After three days of making his way through an underground tunnel escape route, he finally emerged in Tijuana and got through the border to San Diego. Once stateside, he texted his journalism buddy Jesse McMillan the code word. He should be here any minute.

Tony thought about way back when he and Jesse first met in the condo complex in Irvine. That was when Tony was in construction, before he joined the LAPD. He did the math. Thirty years ago. That made him feel old. He was fifty-two but could still pass for forty-five. That had been one of Joanna's complaints. Him thinking he was still young, and still invincible.

A movement at the door had Tony reaching for his gun, holstered under his jacket. When he spotted the tall, slim figure walking toward him, the pile of bricks on his chest lifted. Jesse came loping toward Tony with a grin on his face, his mop of blond hair now streaked with silver. Leave it to Jesse to smile through an operation going sideways after they'd been working on it for a year-and-a-half.

Jesse slid across the booth from Tony. His friend studied him closely before asking, "You okay? That trip through the tunnels sounded like a long one."

"It was tough going, but it worked out. At least my neighbor, Heriberto, will watch over my house for me back there."

"Do you have it?" Jesse asked.

Tony patted his duffel bag. "On a hard drive." He stopped talking when the waitress approached with his plate of food and another brew.

Tony directed his gaze at Jesse. "Something to eat?"

"Can I get a water with no lemon, and a plate of whatever he's having? Looks good."

"Sure, honey," the waitress said, although she kept her eyes on Tony.

When she left, Jesse chuckled.

"What?" Tony asked, raising his eyebrows.

"The ladies are still ignoring me and gobbling you up with their eyes. What do you have that I don't? Dark good looks?"

"Well, you've got a wife who still loves you. That is one thing I don't have." Tony plunked down his beer. "How's Clare doing?"

"Great. She's helping Madeline get settled at UCLA. She got accepted."

Another one of Tony's big failures—not giving Joanna children. "Congrats, man, you must be proud."

"I am, but I kind of wish she'd gone to a school in Orange County where I could keep a better eye on her. But that's just me being an overprotective dad, according to Madeline."

Tony leaned toward Jesse and switched gears. "What's with the operation? How'd the 14K find me in Puerto Vallarta?"

Jesse ran his hand through his hair and sighed. "I'm still waiting on word as to how this all went sideways. In the meantime, my editor is demanding copy."

"I thought you'd been feeding him enough?"

"It's a her. And, yeah, I thought so, too, but she must have sensed something was up when the operation was breached."

"Look, maybe it's time we hung this one up. You've got way too much to lose. It's not like you need the creds with all the stories you've done over the years. How many Pulitzers you have now?"

"Two, but that's not why I'm doing this."

Tony emptied his beer and took a bite of his tacos. After swallowing, he replied, "I know. It's a wrong that does need to be righted. But take it from me. The costs for this stuff aren't always worth it."

"Have you talked to Joanna recently?"

Tony shook his head. "She won't take my calls."

"Sorry, man. But it's not like she didn't understand the life. I know you made your mistakes, but from my vantage point, not all of it was your fault."

Jesse's cellphone vibrated and he checked the display. "Looks like we need to chow down quick. My source is asking for a meeting at a warehouse on twentieth in a half hour."

"I can go in alone," said Tony.

"No way. I'm going with you."

Joanna Molinaro shut her briefcase. She looked around her office and thought about how proud she'd been to get this job five years ago. How excited she was to tell Tony about it. The night they consecrated her desk remained seared into her memory and still made her hot when she thought about it. How she missed his touch. She shook her head to clear it and reminded herself: Tony would never change. Time to erase him from her heart and mind. Maybe with the help of Elliot. They'd only been dating a few weeks, but she liked him, and he had a nice, safe occupation.

"We've got an issue." It was Cara, her assistant.

"What?"

"Members of the 14K are here in San Diego. They were spotted getting off a flight at LAX, originating from Hong Kong, yesterday."

"Do we know why they're here?"

"From intel pulled off the scanner, it looks like they have a meet going down right now at a warehouse on the outskirts of downtown."

Joanna stood and put on her jacket. She unlocked her desk and took out her revolver, sliding it into its holster.

"You need backup," said Cara.

"I know. Have Rodriguez meet me there."

"He's in L.A. today."

"Okay, you come with me."

"Me?" Her assistant's young face, framed by a bob cut, looked both hopeful and doubtful.

"Best classroom is real life. Let's go."

"But I haven't even been given my service revolver yet."

"I'll let Rodriguez know where we'll be. Just bring your computer."

"You got it." Cara scurried out of Joanna's office.

A few minutes later, the two women were headed through afternoon crosstown traffic, Joanna at the wheel and Cara navigating. Joanna smiled to herself as she watched out of the corner of her eye Cara glancing out the window, then back at her phone. Joanna remembered that feeling of the first case in the field. The ping-pong of anticipation in the belly. The fire of fear that licked at the edges. This would be good for her assistant, who she'd seen blossoming since she started training to be an agent at Quantico. A mastermind with computers, Cara promised to be a real asset to the team.

"Depending on their firewalls, I might be able to tap into conversations in the warehouse," said Cara.

"On their cellphones?"

"That, and even what they're saying in there. If someone has a tracker enabled on their phone, I can tap into that."

"Damn, Cara, I'm impressed," said Joanna, glancing at her assistant, already visibly warming to her new role.

It was April in San Diego, and beachgoers lined the beach to their left. Joanna admired the ability to take a day off and get some sun. She was often too nervous and too active to do anything like that. Although, she and Tony had talked about getting a little place by the ocean—maybe in Mexico—and spending their days with their toes in the sand.

There she went again, thinking about her ex, or soon-to-be-ex. The divorce papers still sat in her desk drawer—unsigned by her.

"Take a left turn there." Cara interrupted her thoughts. "The warehouse should be on our right."

Joanna turned and slowed down when she spotted a sprawling industrial building. She pulled the car next to the curb. A fifty-foot security fence surrounded the warehouse, but the gate stood open.

"See if you can pick up anyone talking." Joanna motioned to Cara, who took out her laptop and began pressing keys. After a few minutes, she whispered, "I'm in!"

Both women strained to hear the chatter coming from the computer. Chinese. Joanna knew some.

"Sounds like they're talking about the next shipment and how it's late," she said. "Can you record that?"

"I am," said Cara, looking pleased with herself. "They just said something about the shipment coming in next week, instead. That doesn't appear to be going over well."

Joanna looked at Cara, surprised. "I didn't know you knew Chinese."

Her assistant appeared uncomfortable. "I've been studying it. One of my professors said knowing several languages is a good asset to have."

Joanna was just about to praise her good work when she heard another voice. It sounded American. But they'd just gotten this intel. It couldn't be anyone in her FBI office. Was it a mole?

Joanna glanced at her cellphone. Rodriquez was at least twenty minutes away. She couldn't wait around for his backup and risk not finding out what was going down in there and who the American was. The voices inside seemed to be escalating. It sounded like they were having a hard disagreement. Joanna took out her gun and motioned to the open gate. "I'm going in. Stay here and let Rodriguez know where I am."

Cara appeared startled. "You don't want me to go with you?"

"You're not trained for that. Any idea what part of the building they're meeting in?"

"It must be close, because the signal is pretty clear."

"Keep recording," Joanna ordered. "That's important intel, even if it's not something we can use in court."

Joanna got out of the car and clicked the door shut, then made her way to the gate. Before stepping through, she picked up a stick lying on the ground and threw it through the entrance to the property. No zapped wood. Walking quickly, she entered the property and headed toward the end of the warehouse facing the street.

As she made her way closer to the building, she heard loud voices. Something about the American voice made her pause. Could be someone from the L.A. office, although Joanna thought hers was the only office actively following this latest threat. Her peripheral vision on overdrive, she remained alert as she headed toward the building. When a gunshot rang out, she picked up her pace. Easing up against the warehouse, she listened. Silence at first, and then the sound of doors shutting and a car peeling away.

Keeping her back to the building, Joanna reached over and pushed the door open. Gun outstretched, adrenaline pushed her forward as she made her way inside. Heart pumping in her ears, she spotted an upturned chair, but no sign of anyone. Until someone grabbed her from behind.

3

"Hold on there," said a voice in her ear that sent shockwaves throughout her body. As her mind struggled to make sense of what was happening, he held her close and pulled her out of the building.

When he let her go, Joanna spun around to face Tony. "What—? I thought you were out of the country?"

"I was. Until yesterday."

Joanna noticed Tony sounded short of breath and grimaced as he spoke. She spied blood on his shirt, and her heart jumped into her throat.

"Were you hit?"

"Yeah. The shot knocked me down, and when I got up, everyone was gone. They must have Jesse."

"Your journalist friend?"

"He's not equipped for this."

"What the hell, Tony?"

"Can we talk about this while we look for him? I think they headed out the back of the building."

"You mean, while I look for him."

"I'm going in with you." Tony's jaw was firm. She knew that look.

"You still have ammo in your gun?" Joanna asked him.

"Yeah, I didn't even get a shot off."

They headed back into the warehouse with their guns drawn. No one in the large room. Only a few computer desks and a pile of cardboard boxes in one corner. Pointing her gun to the opposite side of the warehouse where a door stood open, Joanna made her way across the room with Tony following her. When they got to the doorway, Joanna stopped, and they listened. Silence. She motioned with her gun and headed through the door, which led out into a back gravel parking lot. No one there either, but there were tire marks in the gravel, and a gate leading out to the highway stood open.

"No, no, no," groaned Tony, putting his hands on both sides of his head and then dropping them. He gritted his teeth and grabbed his left arm.

"You need a hospital."

"I need to find Jesse."

"If they wanted him dead, they would have shot him and left. What the hell have you gotten yourself into this time?" Joanna demanded, but Tony didn't have a chance to answer. Just then, Rodriguez came rushing towards them from the warehouse door.

"What happened? I had Cara call for backup."

Joanna explained, ending with Jesse's apparent kidnapping. Then glancing up at the side of the building, she added, "If we're lucky, those cameras are working."

Joanna turned to Rodriguez. "Alberto Rodriguez, meet Tony. Tony, Alberto."

Her partner reached out his hand and shook Tony's. "Your reputation precedes you."

Tony's eyebrows shot up. "I can only imagine what that means."

When Rodriguez eyed his shoulder, which oozed blood now, Tony insisted, "I'm fine. I've been shot before. I need to figure out where they took McMillan. Every moment counts with this."

"You're not fine," said Joanna. "I'm taking you to the hospital. Rodriguez has this covered."

Joanna was right. The gunshot wound did need some attention. He could feel the bleeding becoming heavier. As they headed through the warehouse to her car, he stopped walking. "You wouldn't happen to have a tourniquet in your pocket?" he asked.

She turned to look up at him, her brown eyes flickering with something he couldn't discern. "I'll find something. Keep pressure on it until we get to the car."

Cara stood by the car and announced when they walked up, "I got the APB out for Jesse, and they're sending CSI. You okay?"

"I'm fine. But Tony needs attention right away for a gunshot wound."

Cara's eyes went to his shoulder. "Oh, wow, I see that. Want me to take him in?"

"I'll take him," Joanna said abruptly. "I need to question him. Where is that first aid kit?"

Cara went into the car and extracted a first aid kit from the glove compartment. She opened the plastic box and pulled out a large rubber band. "I'm guessing you want a tourniquet?"

"That's perfect," said Tony, taking it from her. "Joanna always said how efficient you are."

Cara smiled. "It's nice to see you, Mr. Molinaro, even if it's under these circumstances."

"Like I've said before, call me Tony."

"Now that we've all gotten reacquainted, how about I tie that tourniquet on you, and we get you to the emergency room?" Joanna pulled the band from his hand and looped it around his arm above the wound in his shoulder. "This will probably hurt."

When she leaned toward him and struggled to tighten the band on his arm, Tony fought the urge to inhale her scent. Restraint, Tony. Stay focused on the task at hand. Once she finished, he got into the passenger seat of Joanna's car. Before he could reach for the door, she slammed it shut.

As they headed to the hospital, neither spoke at first. Finally, Joanna broke the silence.

"You going to tell me what happened back there? Until today, we were just surveilling the 14K, and now all of the sudden you and Jesse are involved in one of the most dangerous Asian gangs out there."

Tony sighed. "Look, I know you're probably not going to believe me, but this isn't my mess. Jesse has been working on this for a long time, and I was just helping by gathering information for him. I set up this sweet surveillance system in a cabin I built in the middle of the Puerto Vallarta jungle."

Tony waited for Joanna's response. Silence, and then she laughed.

"What's so funny?"

"You were minding your own business doing surveillance? Living all by yourself in the middle of the jungle?"

"Okay, maybe doing surveillance isn't exactly minding my own business. And, yes, I live all alone, unless you count my neighbors, Heriberto and his son, Cortez. And the pack of wild boar that comes through now and then. Can you say the same?"

Joanna didn't answer.

"That's what I thought."

"Okay, let's stay focused."

Tony was about to respond when his burner phone buzzed. He reached into his pocket and looked at the screen. *Unknown caller*. Pressing answer, he put the phone to his ear.

Joanna glanced over at him.

"Hello?"

"It's me, Jesse. I'm okay. The 14K members that have me know you're with the FBI right now. It's important you don't let on it's me. The FBI gets anywhere near this, and it won't be good for me. I'll call later with more directions." He hung up.

"Who was that?" Joanna asked.

"I don't know. Bunch of static," Tony said as they pulled up in front of the hospital. "Just drop me off. I'll go in myself."

Joanna started to protest, but Tony got out and slammed the car door, wincing at the pain in his arm as he headed toward the emergency room.

4

Tony marched into the emergency room, seething at the thought of Joanna with someone else. He'd been all alone in the jungle for three years. And she'd been dating?

A nurse stood at the front desk. "Can I help you, sir?"

"Yeah, I have a wound that needs to be taken care of."

The nurse eyed his arm. "A gunshot wound?"

"Yes, a GSW," said Joanna, appearing behind him and flashing her badge. "I'm with the FBI. Can we get this man seen to quickly?"

The nurse nodded and began tapping vigorously into the computer. Then she motioned for them to follow her to a small trauma room. "Take a seat on the bed," she instructed Tony. "Someone will be in shortly to take your vitals. The doctor will be here as soon as he finishes with another patient."

When they were alone, Joanna held up her hand. "You know damn well the doctor has to report a GSW to the authorities. I didn't want this going to the local PD. Better that the FBI signs off on it."

She had a good point. "Thank you," he grunted.

"Does it hurt?"

"Yeah."

"So, about in the car." Joanna shifted in the chair she sat on. "There's not really someone else. Well, there is, but it's really new. He's a dentist."

Tony snorted. Then he stopped himself. "Look, I'm glad you have a new life." He wasn't glad at all, but it sounded good. "Once this mess is sorted out, I'm going to get myself a new life, too."

A nurse entered the room then and smiled at Tony. "We need to get your temperature and blood pressure right now, Mr. Molinaro."

She made a note on her clipboard. Then she inserted an electronic thermometer under his tongue and wrapped the blood pressure cuff on his good arm. After the machine finished taking the reading, she commented, "Your pressure is a little high, but that's to be expected, considering your injury. How is the discomfort level?"

Joanna watched the nurse fawn over Tony and felt immensely irritated. After all this time, she should be used to his effect on women. But she was even madder at herself for caring.

The doctor came in and had Tony lay back on the table as he began cutting the fabric around the wound, using tweezers to pull out material lodged in his skin. Then he cleaned the wound, and while Tony visibly gritted his teeth, extracted the bullet. It clanked as he set it on the tray the nurse held.

"I'll need that for evidence." Joanna instructed her. "We don't want it cleaned or touched in case it has DNA."

The nurse nodded, setting the tray down. "I'll go get a sterile container."

For the next twenty minutes, Tony joked with the doctor as he stitched him up. As Joanna listened to him tell one goofy joke after another, the irritation she had felt earlier drifted away. Tony had a way of using humor to get through any jam. By the time the doctor was done, everyone in the room was smiling.

"You will need to get the stitches taken out in about ten days," the doctor said. "Otherwise, you probably won't have much scarring. I'm giving you antibiotics, as well, to prevent infection."

"Good, I was worried about my pinup modeling gig coming up." Tony sat up from his prone position, his shirt now open, revealing his abs. They were tighter and fitter than Joanna remembered, and the sight made her warm all over. Tony caught her gaze, and she reddened and looked away, glancing down at her cellphone instead.

"Any news?" Tony asked Joanna as the nurse dabbed ointment on his wound and bandaged it up.

"No cameras working in or around the warehouse, unfortunately. We'll know more when we get back to the office after Jay finishes translating the recording we got when you were in there."

"We?"

"You're in my custody now."

"In your custody," said Tony as he stood up, his broad sculpted chest making Joanna feel warm in places she didn't want warm. "I like the sound of that. You got any extra shirts? This one seems to be a goner. Maybe one of your dentist boyfriend's?"

"I don't have any of Elliot's shirts. I told you, this is brand new."

At the front desk, she dealt with paperwork, informing them that the FBI would be picking up the tab.

"Thanks," Tony said as they left the hospital. "But I could have covered my own bill."

"I'm sure you could have, but the paperwork would have taken a lot longer."

On the way to the FBI office, Tony thought about Jesse's cryptic phone call. He sounded okay, but that was Jesse—calm under pressure. It was important that Tony stayed focused and thought this through carefully.

Jesse had said they knew Tony was with the FBI. That meant they were somehow monitoring them, which also meant only one thing. They had someone on the inside of the FBI in Joanna's office. It also meant he was going to need to find a way to ditch Joanna, so he wouldn't compromise Jesse's safety. He knew Joanna, though. She wasn't going to make that easy.

Tony had met Joanna at a crime scene. He had just been promoted to detective after seven years as a beat cop. It was a violent scene. What they originally thought was a home invasion that turned out to be a family squabble. Joanna was crouched down next to the coroner when Tony and his partner arrived. She didn't look up from the conversation but continued speaking in a low voice as they examined the body.

When she finished and stood up, Tony couldn't help but notice how she carried herself—with confidence and a sexy grace. It mesmerized him. She had long black hair she wore in a ropey braid down her back and a beauty mark on her right cheek. Was that lipstick on her lips, or were they naturally that deep red?

"I'm Special Agent Joanna Herrera," she said, smiling into his eyes and extending her hand, which Tony took in his as electric shocks coursed through his body.

"This looks like a home invasion, and it could be related to a chain of them across the West Coast, so we're taking over here," she said.

Tony's partner, a senior agent named Micky Smith, chimed in. "We're of the mindset that this is a local case. So, this is ours."

Tony watched with interest as Joanna crossed her arms over her chest and countered, "We've got a big problem, then."

5

"Tony? My boss has some questions for you."

Tony must have fallen asleep for a minute. He stirred in the chair Joanna had led him to when they got to FBI quarters and grunted.

Joanna stood over him, a concerned look on her face. "You okay?"

"I just need sleep. You got any coffee?"

"You want to lie down for a while?"

"Nah, we gotta get Jesse out as soon as possible."

"We're working on that," said Joanna. "At least let me get you some ibuprofen."

"I'll take that."

As Joanna headed off to get some pain reliever, Tony got to thinking how she looked even better than the day they met. Maturity had a way of doing that with some women.

When she returned with the medicine and a glass of water, he gratefully shook the maximum dose into his hand and washed it down.

"Okay, let's get the questions with your boss over, so I can get out of here. Where is he?"

Joanna put her hands on her hips. "First of all, my boss is a she. Patricia Sumner. Second, you're not going anywhere. You were found at the scene of a crime with a potential foreign threat, and a civilian has been kidnapped."

"Oh, that," said Tony.

Joanna rolled her eyes. "Let's go, Tony."

He followed her through the main office, lined with desks where men and women sat tapping away on their computers. They arrived at an office door that stood open. Joanna rapped on the door frame.

"Come in," called out a voice from behind a large desk. A stately woman stood as they entered, brushing nonexistent creases out of her black pencil skirt. She wore a charcoal blouse and a black jacket hung across the back of her leather chair.

"Special Agent Molinaro, is this the civilian injured at the scene?"

"Yes, ma'am, this is Tony Molinaro. Tony, this is Supervisory Special Agent Patricia Sumner."

Tony reached out to shake her hand, but the woman ignored the gesture. "Go ahead and have a seat." She pointed to the two padded chairs facing her desk.

Sumner looked from Joanna to Tony once they settled. "I assume there's a relation, given the same last name?"

Joanna cleared her throat. "Tony is my ex-husband."

Sumner raised one eyebrow. "Did you know your ex-husband would be at the scene?"

"No, ma'am, we haven't seen each other for a few years."

"Three to be exact," added Tony.

Sumner focused her attention on him. "Can you tell me how you happened to be at an international crime scene involving an Asian Triad our office has been following for more than a year?"

Tony weighed his options before speaking. He knew he had to give the FBI enough real info to make the interrogation go well. He might be sitting in the head honcho's office for what looked like a friendly chat, but Tony knew what this really was.

"I've been helping out my buddy, who's a journalist, Jesse McMillan, with some background research on the 14K Triad. He's working on a big story about it. I used to be LAPD, but I've been on what you could call a sabbatical in Puerto Vallarta, so it gave me something to do."

Sumner leaned back in her chair. "What kind of information were you gathering?"

Tony shrugged and wished he hadn't as pain shot up through his injured shoulder, landing on the side of his head. "Information on their history. Where they operate in the world. That sort of thing."

Sumner leaned forward. "Mr. Molinaro, we have you at the scene of a kidnapping. I'm going to need more information than that if we're going to find your journalist friend." She paused. "Alive."

Tony knew she was trying to scare him into spilling his guts. But he wasn't taking the bait. For all he knew, she could be a mole. He settled on a half-truth.

"For the record, I retired as a detective with the LAPD. Jesse is piecing together an article about the inside workings of the 14K. Looks like he got too close."

Tony watched as Sumner weighed her next words before speaking.

"We need more than the drivel you're giving me. And we need it quick. Anything that could help us find Mr. McMillan."

"My friend is working on something called Operation Ottoman that involves the 14K. There's a group of international journalists working the story together. Their intent was to expose the operation and then turn it all over to you, the feds." Tony wasn't about to tell her the full reason Jesse was digging up dirt on one of the most lethal Asian mafia groups.

"So, we have a case of vigilante justice that could get a group of journalists killed? And you, a former law enforcement officer, are sanctioning this?"

"As mentioned, and for the record, I retired as a detective with the LAPD," said Tony, who could feel disapproval radiating from Joanna in the seat next to him. "Like I said, my friend asked me for some help. Journalists are their own breed. They'll do whatever it takes to make sure the First Amendment is upheld."

Sumner sighed. "I'm well aware of the proclivities of journalists. Give Special Agent Molinaro all the research you dug up. Hopefully, something will point us toward where they're holding Mr. McMillan, and what they want from him."

Tony nodded. "I'll need my duffel bag back. Your team took it at the scene."

Sumner considered for a moment. "I'll call down to evidence and have them release it to you."

When they got back to Joanna's desk, Tony half-expected her to rail him on his irresponsibility regarding Jesse, but she just told him to wait while she got his bag.

He ran through his next moves. He needed to get out of the station and get ahold of his buddy at the CIA. If he could trace the phone Jesse had called on, he might be able to find him and not have to wait for another call. Tony hoped the information they wanted was keeping Jesse safe for now.

When Joanna returned, she dropped the bag at his feet.

"Careful," he exclaimed. "I've got my hard drive in there."

"Good. Let's have it. I want to get it to the cyber lab so they can start downloading your files."

"It'd be better if I went with you to walk them through the download."

Joanna hesitated, then replied, "Fine. Just behave yourself. I don't need any trouble."

Tony reached down for his bag. "I think you're in the wrong profession if you don't want any trouble."

Joanna shook her head and headed toward the elevators.

When the elevator door opened, it was empty. Tony waited for Joanna to get in and then followed.

"How's the pain in your arm?" Joanna asked.

"Not too bad."

"Once we finish with your hard drive, I'll get you settled at a hotel the agency uses. Then you can get some rest."

Tony nodded, but his mind wandered. Was Joanna's dentist friend waiting for her at home?

When the elevator door slid open and they got out, Tony pulled a hard drive out of the duffel bag and handed it to Joanna.

"You can go with me to the lab," she said, taking it. "It's just down the hallway."

"I'll see you there in a minute. I've got to take a whiz."

Joanna hesitated, then looked at the hard drive in her hand. "Bathroom is down the hall to the right, the cyber lab to the left."

Tony waited for Joanna to disappear around the corner before high-tailing it to the door that said Exit. He held his breath when he pushed on the metal release, hoping it didn't trip an alarm. No sound when he passed through into the night, but he knew for certain he was on camera. It wouldn't be long before Joanna discovered he'd slipped out. He had to find transportation fast.

6

Joanna handed the hard drive to the lab tech, Smitty, and sat down on a stool to wait. As he tapped the computer keys, she ran through the crime scene in the warehouse again. It was possible that she missed something that might give them a clue as to where they'd taken Jesse.

After a while, Smitty stopped typing. "You were either played," he said, looking up from his computer at Joanna, "or he accidentally gave you the wrong drive. This has a bunch of video games on it."

"Damn it!" Joanna sprang up. "This is no accident." She should have known better than to think Tony would turn over months of intel that easily. Running out of the lab, she headed straight for the men's bathroom. The room was empty, and Tony was nowhere to be seen. Joanna ran back to the lab and asked Smitty to pull up the security camera on the nearby exit. Sure enough, Tony had slipped out the door and into a cab less than a minute after she'd left him.

"Any way you can get the cab ID number?" Joanna asked.

"Just sent it to your phone with the company's contact info."

"Thanks." She lowered her voice. "Keep this quiet with the boss as long as possible. Hopefully, I can find Tony quickly and bring him back."

On her way to her car, a '68 Camaro that Tony had given her for her 30th birthday, Joanna talked with the cab company dispatcher. A taxi had dropped Tony off at The Hyatt on Mission just two minutes ago. Joanna turned over her car's engine and backed out of the parking lot. As usual, Tony was going rogue, and rogue could get everyone killed.

Tony got out of the cab in front of the Hyatt and started walking toward the Marriott, a few blocks away. Anything he could do to throw Joanna off his trail. By the time he reached the front door of the hotel, his shoulder hurt like a motherfucker. Even though he'd been carrying his duffel bag on the other arm, the pain was more intense than he'd ever felt from a gunshot wound.

At the front desk, Tony asked for a suite. When the red-haired receptionist requested his credit card, he pulled out plastic with the alias Silas Wood.

"Are you visiting the area on business or pleasure, Mr. Wood?" the receptionist asked conversationally as she checked him in.

"A little of both."

She handed him his keycard and smiled. "That's the best kind of trip. Have a great stay."

Inside his suite five minutes later, Tony called down for room service, ordering a burger, fries and a milkshake. Then he opened his bag and checked to make sure the hard drive was still there. It lay at the bottom of his bag wrapped in a Styrofoam sleeve right where he'd left it. When his phone buzzed, he breathed a sigh of relief to see *Unknown caller* on the ID.

"Yeah?

"It's Jesse."

"You okay?"

"For now. They say they'll let me go as long as you bring the hard drive. They want to make sure that you ditched the FBI."

"Yes, I got away from them, and I've got the hard drive. The FBI never saw it." Tony heard muffled voices. "Jesse, you there?"

When his friend came back on the line, Jesse's voice sounded strained. "They want me off the phone. Ten tomorrow morning at 444 Wallace. And come alone."

Tony was about to answer when the phone went dead. He set it down on the desk. The 14K gang wasn't known for being nice. Hopefully handing over the explosive and incriminating information Tony had against them would help him get Jesse out alive.

While he was waiting for room service to deliver his burger, Tony decided to jump in the shower. Taking a plastic bag meant for the ice, he wrapped it around the wound and tied it. Doc said to keep it dry, so he'd do his best.

When Joanna arrived at the Hyatt, she spied the Marriott in the distance. That would be a Tony move. She'd check there first. Continuing until she arrived at the resort hotel, she pulled into the self-parking lot in the back. She slipped on her jacket to hide her holster, took a deep breath and got out of the car.

"Checking into a room, Miss?" The valet asked when she walked through the sliding double doors leading into the lobby.

"No, I'm just collecting someone. I shouldn't be long."

Behind the front desk, a redhead appeared to be texting someone. Joanna cleared her throat and flashed her badge, which made the young girl set down her phone.

"I'm looking for a man who came in about twenty minutes ago. Tall, fifty-ish. He had a duffel bag."

The girl's face lit up and then her eyes widened. "Oh, yes, Mr. Wood. Is he in some kind of trouble?"

"He is in possession of some sensitive information that the FBI needs. Can you tell me which room he is in?"

The girl hesitated.

"This is a matter of national security," Joanna continued, "which trumps your privacy protocols. Just give me his room number, and a keycard to get in, and I'll quietly take care of the rest."

The girl debated for a moment and then took out a keycard and wrote the room number on a slip of paper, handing it to Joanna.

Five minutes later, Joanna stood outside of Tony's room, listening. The shower was running. Good, she could take him by surprise. Just as she was about to insert the keycard, a waiter approached with a room service cart.

"Perfect timing," she said, "that must be my husband's dinner. I can take it in."

The waiter smiled and handed her the check and a pen. Joanna wrote in a generous tip and signed the check, handing it back to him.

He glanced at the amount, and his eyes widened. "Thank you, Mrs. Wood."

"Thank you," she replied. Then as quietly as possible, she slid the keycard through the lock and pushed the cart inside, easing the door shut.

7

Tony got out of the shower and towel-dried, careful to steer clear of his wound. Then he removed the plastic bag and shook an antibiotic pill out of the bottle, popping it in his mouth and washing it down with water. That done, he threw the bathroom door open and walked out into the hotel room.

"Oh, my God, Tony!" Joanna's eyes ran the length of his body, then she looked away, her cheeks turning pink.

"Jo!" Tony thought she might find him, but not this quickly. He reached down and stuffed several fries in his mouth. In between bites, he said, "Well, it's not like you've never seen me naked." Then he picked up the burger and took a big bite. "Man, this is so good. I'd say we can share, but you're probably still not eating red meat. Am I right?"

"Nice job sneaking out of headquarters."

Tony rifled around in his duffel bag and pulled out a pair of gray sweats, putting them on. Then he sat down across from her. "You sure you're not hungry?"

Joanna shook her head but reached for a fry anyway. "I need that hard drive, and you to come back to the office with me."

"I'm definitely not giving away months' of work, just like that. And it's not safe at your office."

"Why is that?"

"Because you've got a mole."

Joanna stopped chewing. "You know this, how?" Was Tony using this information as a diversionary tactic, or did he know something she didn't?

"Just trust me, okay? If I tell you how, that information will go straight back to the 14K."

"Trust you? The man who just ditched me during an investigation?"

"Look, Jo, this is for your own good."

"We're not married anymore, Tony. You can no longer tell me what's for my own good. And don't call me Jo."

"Technically, we are still married. My understanding is you haven't signed the papers yet? Not happy with the deal?"

"I've been busy. We were married for fifteen years. Give me fifteen minutes to review the paperwork."

"It's been eight months since you were served the divorce papers."

"Seriously, Tony, I need that hard drive. My FBI record doesn't need another ding."

Tony raised his eyebrows. "Another ding?"

"It's a long story. I'll tell you when we get back to headquarters."

"I told you. I am not going back there."

Joanna leaned forward, her eyes narrowing. "I don't want to take you in by force, but I will if I have to."

The possibility of Joanna trying to force Tony to leave the room intrigued him. "Do you have handcuffs?" he asked hopefully.

Joanna opened her mouth to reply but stopped when they heard someone at the door. Tony jumped up and grabbed the hard drive and his gun out of the duffel bag. Joanna also pulled her gun. He motioned with his head to the bathroom, and they both went in.

The person who entered was Asian, and he was armed. Tony jumped out of the bathroom and hit him over the head with the butt of his gun. The man fell to the floor, and he turned him over with his foot. "I don't recognize him. You?"

"No, but I'll call this in, and we'll find out."

"I told you, the FBI can't be involved. Take a photo of him, and I'll get a buddy in the CIA to find out who he is."

"I can't just ignore—"

"Jo, seriously, I'm begging you, for Jesse's life. He made it perfectly clear not to involve the FBI."

"You *have* been talking to him. I knew it."

"We've got to get out of here before this guy comes to. Can we go to your place?"

"Sure, I guess so."

Tony threw his stuff together and finished dressing, then grabbed the room service dishes and set them in the tub, turning on the shower. "That'll get rid of our DNA. Wipe the door handles. I cut the wire of the security camera across the hall before I came in and made sure not to touch the elevator buttons."

Once in the hallway, Joanna said, "Let's take the stairs. Less visibility in there, and I think they lead out to the parking lot."

When they arrived at her Camaro, Tony slid in the passenger side and ran his hand along the dashboard. "She's looking good."

"When we get to my place, Tony, you're going to tell me everything."

How Tony infuriated her and excited her all at the same time. Talking her into breaking protocol—breaking the law, even—and leaving a crime scene. It was always the same with Tony. No rhyme or reason, and she found herself following him blindly. Although, she had to admit that he might be on to something. There'd been talk of a mole at headquarters. Everyone in the office had to undergo lie detector tests and an inquiry. Brass said it was just "routine," but Joanna knew better. The big question now was what would she tell her boss? Thanks to Tony she was stuck in the middle.

When they arrived at her bungalow, Joanna drove slowly into the narrow driveway and parked, shutting off the engine.

"Still in your grandparent's place, I see," said Tony.

"I thought you liked this place?"

"I love it. Nothing better than salty sea air to make you feel relaxed. That's why I settled in Puerto Vallarta. Although my cabin is in the jungle near a bunch of waterfalls."

They sat in the car, the sound of the Camaro's engine settling as they looked at the little cottage Joanna's grandparents had left her in their will. Just three blocks from the beach, the place was worth a fortune today.

"Your place in Puerto Vallarta sounds lovely."

"It is, Jo. I wish you could see it. It's got a great view of the jungle, and it all runs on solar power. I installed a satellite, too, and the insulation is primo. Keeps the muggy air out. Took me months to get it just right."

"Do you ever wonder what things would have been like if you stayed in construction?"

"I've thought about it," Tony admitted. "I've always loved building things with my own hands, and it takes a lot of thought and planning. But I got bored with it as a job after a while. That's why I became a cop."

Joanna remained silent.

"What you really mean is, what would things have been like for us, if I'd stayed in construction. Don't you?" Tony asked.

Joanna nodded her head slowly in the dark car.

8

When they walked into the house, Tony recalled other times when he came through the doorway, and his heart lifted—no matter what crap had been flung at him that day. He wanted to inhale deeply. The scent of home.

He pointed at the flowers on the living room table. "You grow those?"

"No," Joanna said, putting her things down. "Do you want something to drink?"

Tony was ripped back to reality. "They must be from your dentist friend."

Joanna was silent.

Tony cleared his throat. "You got any beer?"

"No, just some chardonnay."

"I'll take a glass, if you don't mind." Tony eased himself onto the sofa, careful not to jostle his arm. He glanced around the living room. Just like he remembered it. A collection of eclectic artwork hanging on the walls by Joanna's nieces and nephews, the multicolored afghan her mother made draped over the side of the old, comfy couch. The only thing missing were the photos of him and Joanna that used to sit on the mantel.

Joanna brought a glass of wine to him and sat at the other end of the couch with her own glass. She had taken off her shoes and put on the fluffy around-the-house socks he remembered.

"Are you going to tell me what's really going on, Tony?" She pulled her legs up and sat cross-legged against the end of the couch.

Tony took a big swallow of the wine and waited for it to settle like fire in his belly. "I don't want to put you in danger, Jo."

Joanna blew out an exasperated breath. "I'm an FBI agent, Tony. Last month, I helped take down a Russian human trafficking ring. The month before that we raided a meth lab. I navigate danger just about every day."

Tony gazed at the wine in the glass and swirled it, wondering. Did Joanna and her dentist friend sit and talk like this after a long day?

"Tony? What are these people into?"

He leaned back on the couch. "Their reach is far, and what they're into is lucrative and deadly."

Joanna sat up. "Weapons? Explosives?"

Tony shook his head. "No, not that kind of deadly."

Joanna slammed her wine glass down, the contents slopping over the edge and running along the stem onto the wooden coffee table. "Damnit," she muttered, going into the kitchen and returning with paper towels. Once she soaked up the mess, she collapsed back onto the couch and put her head in her hands. Then she looked at him, strain in her brown eyes. "It's always like this with you, Tony. Everywhere you go."

Tony drank the rest of his chardonnay and stood up. "I appreciate you agreeing to let me stay here, but let's face it. It's not in your best interest. If I go now, the worst the FBI will get you on is losing me. Much better than harboring a fugitive."

"Where will you go?"

Tony reached for his duffel bag. "I'll figure something out. I always do."

"Stay," she said, standing up to face him. "It's late, and we're both tired. I'll call into the office and tell them I lost you, but that I have an idea where I can look for you in the morning. That'll buy us—you, some time."

Tony sat back down, relieved. The thought of sleeping on a park bench tonight didn't sound good.

When Joanna hung up after an ass reaming from her boss, her phone started to ring again. Elliot. She hit ignore and headed back into the living room. As she entered the room, she started to speak, but Tony was already asleep. Picking up the afghan her mother made, she stood over him with the blanket clasped in her arms and smiled. For all his irritating habits, and the hailstorm that broke out when he was around, she felt a sense of peace having Tony back in the house. Gingerly, she placed the blanket over him and tiptoed out of the room.

"Are you going to ask me for my number?" Joanna said.

They had finished butting heads over who had jurisdiction over the home invasion crime scene. The FBI had been given lead, and Tony's partner was on the phone complaining to their boss.

"I was getting to it." Tony gave Joanna an easy smile.

"Better get to it faster. I'm leaving any minute."

"Give me your phone."

"It's government property."

Tony laughed. "I'll put my number in it."

"Give me your phone. You're supposed to call me, anyway."

"A traditional gal. I like that," he said, handing over his cellphone.

Joanna tapped her number into Tony's contacts and handed the phone back to him. "I'm traditional alright. Raised by a Mexican mother and father."

"Second-generation?"

"That's me. You?"

"Raised by a second-generation Italian mama on the East Coast. But I've been living in SoCal my adult life."

"And your father?"

"A casualty of the Vietnam War. I was a baby when he died."

"Sorry to hear that." Joanna's eyes softened. "That must have been hard as a kid."

His partner hung up the phone and chimed in. "What's hard?"

"Navigating the traffic when you're trying to get across town here in L.A.," Tony answered.

"Speaking of, we better get going."

Tony winked at Joanna as they left.

Joanna took a shower, washing off the day. As she lathered up, she thought about Tony's reticence regarding sharing information about Jesse. Had he gotten himself involved in something he couldn't climb out of? What was he hiding?

By the time she toweled off, Joanna had decided. She would take Tony into the office in the morning. They could set him up with a wire before he went in to get Jesse. That way they'd have a better chance of getting them both out safely. Not to mention, save her job. She'd screwed up big time eight months ago. A perp almost killed her partner, because she was distracted. She'd given the excuse that she was worried about her mother being in the hospital, but that wasn't it. She'd been reeling from getting the divorce papers from Tony.

She remembered fuming. How dare he serve her with papers when she was the one who had ended things? She had stuffed the papers in her desk drawer where they still remained.

Now she was dating a wonderful, kind man. He spent his free time being a big brother to several kids and did free monthly dental work at a clinic. He was the man she always wished Tony could be. Secure, steady and stable. With Tony in the next room, though, there was one more adjective that came to mind regarding Elliot. Boring.

9

Tony woke at six in the morning and checked his phone. Nothing from Jesse. There was no way Joanna was going to let him walk out the door. That meant getting out of here quietly in the next few minutes. He hated to leave—especially when they were finally talking.

He stole into the kitchen and found a caffeinated soda in the fridge. Diet, of course, but it'd do the trick. Covering the can with a towel to muffle the sound, he pulled the tab, then downed it quickly, wiping his mouth with the back of his hand. No point in writing a note. He wouldn't know what to say. He never did when it came to Joanna. It always felt like someone had reached into his mouth and literally tied his tongue. Back in the living room, he went for his bag, but it was gone.

"Son of a bitch."

"Looking for this?" said Joanna, flicking on the lights and momentarily blinding him. She held his bag in her hand.

"Jo." Tony slowly approached her. "Just let me go deal with Jesse."

"I can't. If something happens to you and/or Jesse, it'll be my fault."

"You won't even be there."

Tony reached for his bag, but Joanna pulled it behind her. "For once in your life, do the sensible thing and let the FBI help you. Aren't you getting a little old for rogue?"

"Shit, Joanna, rogue has saved my ass every time. Just give me a head start, and then tell them I outran you."

"That would make me look like an idiot, and I'm not. I've grown in my career these past three years you've been away. I'm a damn good agent." Joanna had a catch in her voice that got Tony's attention. "This time, I'm doing what I think is best."

Irritation overtook Tony. "What do you want, Jo? Really. What's this all about?"

Joanna didn't blink. "It's about you trusting me with information and to take care of myself and make the right decisions."

Tony weighed her words. She *had* changed. The old Joanna wasn't this direct and sure of next steps. Finally, he spoke. "Okay, fine. We've been working for months to break a counterfeit prescription drug ring run by the 14K. The meds are laced with trace amounts of mercury and other really dangerous substances. Kids and adults all over the West Coast are taking the fake meds for conditions like diabetes and asthma, and they're being poisoned and even killed."

"How is you getting killed trying to extract Jesse going to help this? Especially if you hand over the evidence they're looking for?"

"It'll be a lot worse if the mole at your headquarters gets wind of things. You can't tell me there hasn't been chatter at the FBI about a mole."

The look on Joanna's face told him everything.

"I just know the brass is looking, and our office is being scrutinized," she said, finally.

Tony understood she was in a tough spot. And he knew he didn't always need to manage and control things—their marriage counselor had told him that.

"Would you come as my backup, if I asked you to?" Tony said.

Joanna appeared surprised and even pleased. "Yes, if kids are involved. And if someone on my team is dirty, you're right, it's too risky to trust them."

"Great. But can we not knock heads over every decision? Will you promise to trust me?"

"If you promise me you won't bolt again."

"I promise."

"When and where are you supposed to meet them to get Jesse?"

"Ten this morning at a building on Wallace. I have to make a couple calls first that can help us. The first one to a buddy at the CIA."

"I've got a secure line in my bedroom."

When Tony walked through the threshold of Joanna's room, he noted the covers flung back on the right side where she liked to sleep. A book lay open on the other side of the bed. She picked up the receiver of a land-line on the night table and handed it to him. Tony punched in the number and waited.

"Hammerstein."

"Hey, Troy, it's me, Tony."

"Long time no talk. What's up?"

"I'm back in the States. On an informal case. Involving the 14K."

Hammerstein laughed. "Only you would refer to a case as informal when it comes to a group of thugs like the 14K."

"Long story. I'll tell you sometime over a drink or three."

"How can I help?"

"Any word on a member getting knocked out at a local hotel last night? I know your agency has a finger on the pulse of every wiretap in town."

Hammerstein chuckled. "I'm not sure about every wiretap, but close. Not the line you're on now, though, it's secure. Name is Xuong Chang. He's an enforcer for the 14K. Mid-level. He was tasked with shutting down an operation building a case against one of their ventures—contraband pharma, but he got a concussion last night instead. Know anything about the counterfeit drugs operation? A little quid pro quo?"

It was Tony's turn to laugh. "Yeah, currently the 14K is in the market for months' worth of intel on that operation."

"Anything you can give us from those months?"

"I'm close to figuring out who the leader of the pharma ring is."

"Now that info I can sink my teeth into."

"I'll be in touch." Tony hung up the phone.

Joanna opened the bedside table and extracted her laptop. "Well? What did he say about the guy in the hotel?"

"He's a mid-level enforcer. Xuong Chang is his name. I'm kind of hurt they didn't send in the big guns."

Joanna smirked. "You'll get over it. Now what?"

"I'll call my informant. See what scuttlebutt he can share."

Tony dialed Twitch's number and waited for several rings until he picked up. There was silence on the other end of the line.

"It's me, Tony. You screening your calls now?"

"Tony, man, what up? How's Mexico?"

"I'm back in San Diego right now. I need to meet with you on Wallace. In an hour. Not too hungover, I hope."

"I quit drinking, man. Been on the straight and narrow for six months."

"Fantastic, congrats."

"There's a diner on the southwest corner of Wallace. Aunty Mae's. I like the hash browns."

When Tony hung up, Joanna said, "Damn it!" She snapped the lid closed on her laptop. "I was checking my email. Sumner is demanding that I bring you back by this afternoon. Or I can turn in my badge."

"We find Jesse; I'll make an appearance at your office."

"You'd do that?"

"Of course. My priority is saving Jesse. When that's done, I'm all yours."

10

Joanna pulled open a drawer and contemplated what to wear. She weighed her options. Jeans and a blouse would probably be best.

"Remember that place we used to go for lasagna?"

"Mario's?" Joanna set the jeans on the bed. "That restaurant burned down last year."

"That's a bad omen." Tony looked visibly upset. "We went there on our first date."

Joanna felt her heart clutch at the memory, then she shook it from her head. "I don't have a bulletproof vest your size."

"I've got some Kevlar I'm going to slip into my jacket," said Tony. "I'll let you get dressed."

After he left the room and shut the door, Joanna sat on the bed steadying her breath, the memory of that first date overcoming her.

She'd been downright giddy getting ready. By the time she decided on the perfect outfit, she had taken everything out of her closet. She remembered her final choice well. An electric blue clingy dress with spaghetti straps. It hugged her hips and stopped just above the knee. She would never forget the look on Tony's face when she opened the door. A mixture of puppy dog and panther.

Over dinner at Mario's that night, Tony regaled her with one hilarious story after another of his antics as a kid.

"So, my mama has this pasta press that she got from my grandpa. He's old school, so it's a relic. She told me never to touch it. Of course, never is an invitation when you're a ten-year-old boy. One day there was a school holiday, and I had to stay home alone. I took out the pasta machine and used it to make ribbons and shoestrings with my playdough."

Joanna laughed. "What happened with the pasta press?"

"I guess I didn't clean the machine too well. Mama made pasta a few weeks later, and the fettucine noodles ended up having stripes of pink and yellow playdough in them." Tony laughed heartily. "What about you? Any stories?"

"I don't know if it's as funny, but here's one. My parents are traditional Mexicans, and they were okay with my brothers going to college, but they didn't see the point in me attending. I needed to go, though, to get into the FBI."

"What'd you do?"

"This sounds so crazy when I say it out loud. But I had an office job at a local law firm during the day. So, I went to night school for six years, and they never knew."

"What did they think you were doing?"

"I told them I was going out with my girlfriends at night. Presumably to find a husband so I could settle down and start having babies."

Tony laughed. "That is crazy. But I get it. Parents want to protect their kids. It comes from the right place."

Joanna liked his answer.

When Tony dropped her off in front of her apartment door after dinner, he touched the tip of his finger to her beauty mark. "You're gorgeous, you know." He then reached down and brushed his lips across hers, then kissed her deeply. So deeply, she felt the impact clear to the ends of her fingertips and toes. When they came up for air, they were both breathing hard. Joanna wanted him to come inside.

As if he read her mind, Tony said, "Next time."

"Who says there's going to be a next time?"

"You, of course." He motioned with his head to her door and smiled. "Go inside now. I want to make sure you get home safely."

Completely flustered by this point, her lips burning from the kiss, Joanna turned and somehow managed to get the key into the door and let herself in, leaning against it once she got inside. After she regained her bearings, she peered through the peephole. Tony's car was gone.

The tapping on her bedroom door snapped Joanna to attention. "You about ready?" Tony called out.

"Yes!" She slipped out of her pajama bottoms and slid on the jeans. When she walked out into the living room a few minutes later, her bullet-proof vest and gun were well-concealed under her jacket.

"You look ready," he said. "And, Jo?"

"Yes?"

"Thank you. Jesse's the brother I never had. I'm glad you're going to have my back."

"It's my job."

"And you're good at it. I see that." He put the hard drive under his arm as they left the house and headed for the Camaro.

Twenty minutes later, they pulled up to the diner, which looked more like a dive. When they got out of the car, though, the food smelled heavenly to Tony.

"This guy is a little antsy, and probably a lot cagier now that he's not using. But he usually has some good intel that has gotten me out of jams."

"Or into them," Joanna added.

"Point taken."

They entered the diner, and he spotted Twitch at the back of the building near the exit. His informant stood up when he saw them coming. He looked at Joanna with questions in his eyes.

"She's not interested in whether you're keeping up your appointments with your parole officer."

"She's FBI," said Twitch.

"Like I said, don't worry about it. Trust me. Hey, staying clean looks good on you." Tony had never seen Twitch's eyes so clear. He even wore a clean t-shirt and board shorts. Nails still bitten to the quick.

They all sat down as the waitress approached.

"What can I get you all?" she asked.

"A double order of hash browns?" Tony pointed to Twitch. "I'll have some eggs over easy and bacon. A pot of black coffee, too."

Joanna ordered a fruit bowl and cottage cheese, and Twitch added eggs to his potatoes.

Once the waitress walked out of earshot, Tony put his arms on the table and leaned forward. "Tell me everything you know about the 14K, what they're up to, their local spots, their firepower."

Twitch glanced at Joanna again.

"Pretend she's not here."

Twitch looked anxiously around. "An office building on Wallace is their main place. It's where they keep their weapons. They also have a couple of drugstores. One on Fourth and the other on Mission."

"Does the leader ever show up for any of the buys or meets?"

Twitch eyed the waitress headed their way with plates piled on both arms.

"He's more of a phantom. Unless something important is going down, then he's there." Twitch stopped talking until the waitress had set their plates down and left.

"You ever seen him?" Tony continued.

Twitch shook his head. "No, but I heard him. He has a weird voice."

"Weird how?"

"Hard to explain. High-pitched, you know. Like I said, weird."

"How do the 14K play with the local Mexican mafia?"

"They don't. Word is they took out half of the local Mexican gang last month. Raided their headquarters. They're cleaning up."

"To move in."

Twitch nodded. "Look, I know you don't need me telling you what to do. But be careful. This is big time. They've got an arsenal of guns across the border in TJ. There's also some underground tunnels that the Mexicans made and have been using, but word is the 14K are going to take them over soon."

That could be a big problem, thought Tony. Given that one of those tunnels ran straight to his home in Puerto Vallarta.

11

They pulled up in front of the building on Wallace, and Tony shut the car off. "My plan is to trade Jesse for the hard drive. Then we bolt."

"Just like that? I thought you worked months on that information?"

"I did, but my focus right now is getting Jesse out. You ready?" he asked, his eyes analyzing her, concerned.

"Yes, Tony, I am. I've had more than ten years in the field. I know what I'm doing."

"I know you do."

They got out of the car and walked toward a one-story building with corrugated metal siding that sprawled across half the block. At the steel front door, Tony rapped several times and stood back when a burly Asian guy appeared and scowled at them.

"We're here for the trade."

When the man moved to check Tony for weapons, he said, "Of course, I'm armed. And so is she. You touch our firepower; I blow this hard drive to smithereens."

The guard shouted something in Chinese behind him, then moved back to let them in. They came face-to-face with three more men training rifles on them.

"No need for the warm welcome. We just want McMillan," said Tony.

"We're prepared to leave the hard drive, but only after we have him. Otherwise, I'm going to shoot the shit out of it."

"Let them pass," called out a voice. The trio parted to reveal a medium-built man wearing a black suit. He was mid-forties, with flecks of silver in his black hair, and held an unlit cigar in one hand.

"No one told you to bring the FBI, Mr. Molinaro."

"She's here as a friend," Tony shot back. "We want to see McMillan."

The man stared at Tony, unblinking. "And you are prepared to fulfill your end of the bargain? That hard drive you are holding contains the valuable information we want?"

"Yes. It's all yours once I have my friend."

The man then called into the shadows, "Bring him out." There were stacks of boxes behind him and pallets containing what looked like munitions. A guard yanked Jesse from the shadows and pushed him forward with the butt of his gun. The front of Jesse's shirt was bloody, and his face looked bashed up.

"Our information?" asked the man.

"Who am I giving it to?"

The man smiled. "I am the boss's envoy. He sends his apologies. He couldn't make it."

"Let McMillan leave with her. Then I'll give you the hard drive."

"No tricky business, as you Americans say. You live by your word, or we will kill everyone you know."

"Your reputation is well known," said Tony. "All the information is on this drive. We just want to get out of here in one piece."

"I would say you are a wise man, Mr. Molinaro. But only time will tell regarding that."

The guard approached with Jesse, and Tony said to Joanna, "Get him to the car." She nodded as they walked out together, Jesse moving with a slight limp.

The man came closer, his eyes glinting of metal. "You are a brave man, or you are a fool, I know not what."

"I'm going to hand this over, and then I'm going to leave," Tony said, lowly and evenly. "If something happens to me when I do, you won't be getting the encryption key. Good luck trying to retrieve the data without it."

"You've made your point, Mr. Molinaro." The man remained outwardly calm, but Tony could feel a ripple of tension coming from him. Tony handed over the hard drive, then backed out of the building, ready to draw his gun if necessary. Once outside, he ran to the Camaro, and Joanna sped them away.

"You okay, Jesse?" Tony turned to the back seat to get a good look at his friend.

"A few broken ribs, and I'm going to have a black and blue face, but I'll survive. Thanks for getting me."

"Shit, I had to. Clare would never forgive me."

Jesse started to laugh but stopped, his face screwing up from the pain.

"But, seriously, Jesse, you know I'd never leave you. Not my brother from another mother."

"I appreciate that, and so does Clare."

"You want to see a doctor?" Tony asked Jesse.

"No, just get me on the train back to Orange County. Clare can bandage me up. If you have a shirt I could wear, though, that would be cool. I don't want to scare everyone on the train."

Reaching into his bag, Tony pulled out a clean t-shirt and handed it to Jesse.

"Thanks for all of the hard work over the last year and half, Tony," said Jesse. "I'm sorry it's not going to be put to good use, but I think I might be getting a little too old for this. I'd like to be around for Madeline's college graduation."

"I hear you," said Tony as he checked the passenger side mirror for a tail just as his phone buzzed. Answering, he barked into it, "I'll send the encryption key when I'm safe, in ten minutes." Then he hung up and leaned back in his seat, breathing a sigh of relief.

After they dropped Jesse off at the train station, Joanna asked, "So, what's our story about what went down today? And you are going into headquarters with me to give a formal statement like you said you would, right?"

"Yes, as promised," said Tony. "Story will be that you caught me getting Jesse, and I'd already traded the information."

"They're not going to be happy about that. They'll probably grill you on the details of what you handed over."

"I'll tell them it was just background work for Jesse's articles. I'll talk my way out of it."

"This is all way too easy. They give you Jesse. You give them the information you spent months gathering." Joanna shook her head. "Why do I feel like the other shoe is going to drop, and it's going to be like a chunk of granite?"

"I don't know, Jo, maybe the work has you jaded."

"I'm still thinking about how this is all too pat. And you're so calm about this. Since when do you give up righting a wrong this easily?"

"Maybe I'm revising my priorities like Jesse. Realizing there's more to life than vigilante justice."

Joanna pulled into headquarters and shut off the car's engine.

"What are you going to do after we finish at headquarters today, if they don't throw you in jail?"

"I could stick around, if you want me to." Tony watched Joanna's face for a reaction, but as always, she was impossible to read.

12

As Joanna had predicted, her colleagues—especially her boss—were fuming about the fact that Tony gave the 14K his intel. He kept insisting it was just background to Jesse's articles. To appease them, he shared the information Twitch had given him on the drugstore locations.

As he bullshitted his way through the conversations, Tony couldn't help thinking about having to leave Joanna. Just when she was at least talking to him again. But what he had to do next would compromise her job even further. She clearly loved her work at the agency. He didn't want to put her job in any more jeopardy. Better to fly solo from here on out.

He refocused on the conversation when Sumner said, "That's all you have to say, Mr. Molinaro?"

"I guess at this point you're not going to call me Tony. Yep, that's it. My shoulder is hurting pretty bad, so I'd like to get out of here and get some pain reliever."

Sumner sighed. "You realize I could hold you on suspicion of treason?"

"I get that."

"But I know you've given us all you're going to. We'll be keeping an eye on you, so watch your step."

"I always do." Tony stood up.

Joanna walked into the room then. "Done?"

"For now," said Sumner. "I want a report on my desk by morning."

"Yes, ma'am." Joanna followed Tony into the hallway. "I'll walk you out."

When they got to the parking lot, Tony looked up to see a handful of stars in the night sky. "Too much light pollution here," he commented. "You should see the sky in Puerto Vallarta."

"That's all you're going to say?"

"What else do you want me to say? We both know you want me gone, so you can go back to your life. I'm thinking you take me to rent a car. I can drive back to Mexico."

"So, you're leaving?"

"You're not giving me much choice."

"Tony, stop the doublespeak. For once in your life be honest with me."

Tony thought for a moment as he looked into her expectant eyes. "Okay, I need to go back to Mexico for the intel I hid there. That's my insurance policy. I handed over only a portion of what I gathered. But the 14K are going to start suspecting I have more. I don't have much time."

Joanna was a combination of elated and furious. Then she realized she didn't want to let him go. Not yet. There were still so many things left unsaid.

She started toward her Camaro, pulling her keys out of her pocket and holding them up for Tony to see. "I had the auto shop install power doors and locks in the car, for safety," she said. "That way if I'm ever being followed, I'm not fumbling to get the key in the lock."

"Great idea," said Tony. "Does it reach very far?"

Joanna stopped walking. "Yeah. From several yards away. Watch," she said, pressing the remote.

The blast was instantaneous, throwing Joanna against Tony as they skidded backward and fell against the pavement. Pieces of her car flew through the air, a hubcap spinning past them.

Tony sprang to his feet and reached down for Joanna's hand. Nearby car horns began sounding all around them. He grabbed her up and against his chest. "We need to get out of here. Now." He pulled her with him toward a main thoroughfare, slipping into and through a crowd gathering on the street. After they'd rushed along for several blocks, Tony slowed.

"What now?" he said, looking at her.

Joanna pressed her lips tightly together. There was no perfect solution.

"How about heading to your place in the jungle? You need to get the intel, and we can lay low there."

"That's exactly what I was just thinking," said Tony. "We can rent a car under an alias and drive there."

"But I should really call the office," Joanna burst out.

"Hell, you should! That bomb was in your car. It's best they think we're dead right now so we can figure out who the hell wants you or us dead."

Maybe Tony was right. And in fact, running away with him gave her a ripple of excitement. It'd been a long time since she felt this excited about a case—or anything.

When Twitch picked them up a little while later, he complained, "Twice in one day, man? I'm missing an AA meeting."

"Sorry to threaten your sobriety, but this is life and death."

"It always is with you, Tony." Twitch took a cigarette out of a packet and lit up.

Joanna smiled at Twitch's comment. Seems she wasn't the only one to get dragged around by Tony's capers.

"Just get us to Hertz Rental downtown," said Tony.

Twitch took a deep toke of his cigarette, flicking ashes out the window whenever he waited at a stoplight.

"I won't be asking you for help for a few days," added Tony. "Make sure and answer the phone, though."

As he drove, Twitch played a rhythm on the steering wheel, taking puffs on his cigarette in between.

A minivan seemed to be the most inconspicuous vehicle they could get. They drove it to Joanna's bungalow and parked several houses away, slipping in the front door as quickly as possible.

"You got a go bag?"

"Of course. I'll get it and throw in some bottled waters and snacks for the road. How long do you think before the FBI come to search the house?" Joanna asked.

"My guess is a few hours," Tony said. "Let's prep to go, then get a half-hour of shuteye. We'll be in much better shape to drive all the way to Mexico tonight."

Joanna threw a bunch of granola bars into her go bag, along with bottles of water and some apples and oranges. Then she unplugged her laptop and slid that into the top. "If they come while we're napping," she said, zipping it closed, "we can always go into the panic room." She and Tony had the room put in several years ago adjacent to their bedroom— just in case. Joanna never imagined she'd use it to hide from the FBI. It was only the size of a closet, but they could squeeze in if they had to.

They went into Joanna's bedroom and each lay down on the bed, their bags on the floor beside them. Within a minute of laying down, Joanna heard him lightly snoring. She smiled at the ceiling, soon feeling herself drifting off.

The sound of the doorbell ringing in the early morning hours woke them. Joanna pressed the remote for the saferoom. She sprang up and grabbed her bag, entering quickly, Tony right behind her. Just as the door slid shut, she heard the sound of voices and footsteps coming through the front door.

"I have to say this was one of our smartest moves, soundproofing this escape hatch," said Tony quietly.

"It was." Joanna agreed, becoming unnerved at their closeness. Wedged together in the small space, she could feel Tony's heart pumping.

13

Pressed close to Joanna in the tiny closet, Tony could feel the heat of her body, smelled her favorite perfume, a blend of rose and ylang-ylang. He tried to control himself, but the same desire he always felt when he was near her surged through him. He allowed a hand to drift across her back, letting it come to rest at her waist. She looked up, then relaxed against him. Without thinking, he lifted her chin and leaned down to let his lips brush against hers, then kissed her deeply. To his delight, she didn't hesitate and kissed him back. Like the kisses he remembered when their passion lasted all through the night. As they kissed, Joanna's arms wrapped about his neck. He moved his hands under her blouse and undid her bra, his fingers running across the hardness of her nipples. Reaching down to undo the buttons on her jeans, he slid his hand into her pants, his fingers finding the softness of her, already swollen and moist. Her reaction was intense. She urged him deeper into her, which he did, his desire ramping up until he found it hard to breathe.

"Don't stop, Tony," her breath was warm against the skin of his neck. Her fingers wrapped around his upper arm with a strength that surprised him.

At the same time, she eased his zipper down and released his penis; it quickly grew strong and hard in her hand.

"Joanna, Joanna," he breathed. "I miss you so much." He heard a muffled cry as she pressed her face against his chest as she came.

Her reaction made him frenzied. She responded by clasping him between her hands. He could feel his heart throb in his penis. He wanted her to never let go and held his breath, struggling to stay quiet as her fingers moved up-and-down, up-and-down, until he exploded in her hands.

"I'm sorry," he breathed, burying his face in her hair.

"Don't be," she said, taking a tissue from her pocket and wiping everything away. She looked up and smiled and then kissed him, their tongues entwined, warm and sweet in one another's mouths, until Tony could no longer think.

His heart thudding in his ears, they held one another when a sudden noise sounded from the other side of the door. "*Shh*," he held a finger to his lips. "There's an intercom." He reached over and turned a knob. "We can turn it on to see if they're still here." Footsteps leaving the room and heading down the stairs, and then silence on the other side.

They waited another five minutes, then slid the saferoom door open.

"They're still probably watching the house, so let's leave out the back door," said Joanna.

"Got any disguises laying around, by chance?" asked Tony.

Joanna walked into her room. They had upended a few things, but it wasn't too much of a mess.

"Remember the Halloween we dressed up as Marge and Homer Simpson?"

Tony chuckled. "I don't think Marge's blue hair is what we want right now. What about the time you were Marilyn Monroe?"

Joanna's eyes lit up. She slid open the closet door and pointed to a hat box on the top shelf.

Tony brought it down and pulled out a blonde wig.

"Perfect," she said, struggling to get her thick head of black hair under the wig. "Not bad," she said to her reflection in the mirror.

When they got downstairs, Joanna was relieved to see the place wasn't too trashed. She and Tony peered out the back door and didn't see anyone, so they made their way through her neighbors' backyards to the minivan. Tony threw their belongings into the back seat, then they got in and quietly pulled away from the house.

Joanna leaned back, easing out a big sigh.

"How you holding up?" asked Tony.

"Just reeling a bit. Having a hard time wrapping my head around the fact that someone in my office—on my team—might have tried to kill me."

"Betrayal sucks."

"How long to your cabin?" asked Joanna, changing the subject.

"It'll take us about twenty-five hours to drive there. You can get some sleep if you want to."

Joanna nodded. She watched Tony expertly maneuvering the car, checking in the rearview mirror and peripherally, constantly as he drove. She had forgotten how impressed she'd always been with his multitasking. Now that she thought about it, there were many things he did well that maybe she hadn't acknowledged when they were married.

"Roses aren't going to make up for it, Tony. Just let me stew."

He had given her a big vase of roses at midnight on Valentine's Day, or as he pointed out, 11:59.

"I thought you might say that, so I bought you chocolates, as well," he said, pulling out a big box of her favorites.

"You don't get it. It was you I wanted here tonight." Her face was tearstained. She sat at the dining room table amidst a proverbial meal not eaten.

"I'm sorry. But we were going to lose the guy if we didn't intercept him at the airport."

Joanna sighed deeply, pushing a plate of steak away and putting her head on the table.

"Maybe third time is the charm?" she heard him saying.

Joanna lifted her head to see Tony holding out a small box. She reached out and took it.

"This won't get you off the hook," she said, opening it to a gorgeous heirloom pearl necklace.

"That was my grandma's. My mom told me to give it to you for one of our special anniversaries. I figured our tenth Valentine's Day is perfect."

Joanna lifted the necklace into the light of the dining room chandelier. "It's lovely, Tony," she said, sighing.

When they approached the Tijuana border, Tony asked, "Can you get out our passports?" Joanna was perplexed.

"I've got one for you, too. In my duffel bag."

She unzipped the bag, extracting the passports and flipping them both open to look at the names. "Jane and Tim Hanson. Why do you have a passport for me?"

"I had it made that last year when we were married, when all the shit was hitting the fan with that last case." He glanced at her with an almost guilty look.

Joanna reached out and touched Tony's arm. "Thank you."

"Anything for you, Jo. I'm always here."

"I know that," she said quietly. Fact was, she'd always known that. But now, she finally believed it.

14

As Tony navigated the minivan through the congested streets of Tijuana, the smell of diesel and exhaust choked the air.

"The drive smells better once we get out of the city," he commented. "The air is even fresher when we get closer to Puerto Vallarta, but that won't be until tomorrow."

"They've probably figured out by now that we weren't in the car." Joanna glanced out the window at downtown Tijuana. The mishmash of primary colors on the storefronts reminded her of a jumbled box of crayons. "I'm going to miss that car."

"Remember the day I gave it to you?"

Joanna laughed at the memory. "The keys were in the bottom of the cereal box. How could I forget."

"Those were some fun days. I can't believe it's been fifteen years."

Joanna willed back tears as she thought about how excited she'd been on that birthday. On their first date, she had told him she liked vintage cars, especially Camaros. When he presented her with one of her own, she'd been thrilled.

"I bet I could find you another one."

Joanna smiled. "How about we deal with this op. Then maybe I'll take you up on the offer. But I want blue next time, instead of red."

Tony looked at Joanna. "Yeah, why?"

"I feel like it suits me better, now that I'm forty-five."

"You're still young, Jo."

She sighed and leaned back. "Why do I feel so old, then?"

"You're just tired. Take a nap."

Joanna closed her eyes.

As he drove, Tony glanced at Joanna while she slept. God, it was good to have her here with him. Though he'd been miserable without her these past years, he hadn't realized how deep the sadness went. If he was honest with himself, he'd been living a half existence. He wondered if Joanna would go back to her life once this was over, and to her dentist. Well, for now he had her to himself.

All afternoon, they traveled through the Sonoran Desert. Tony knew this drive well. Miles of dusty terrain pockmarked with cactus and tumbleweeds. The dry air settled into him, making his nose dry and his lips crack.

"Want a water bottle?" Joanna asked.

"You read my mind."

She reached into her bag. "I can drive whenever you want to nap."

"Maybe we stop for the night in Hermosillo. There's a handful of decent hotels. Then we can power through until we reach the cabin tomorrow."

"You think it's a good idea to stop?"

"I figure Hermosillo is far enough off the radar for one night. I doubt the FBI will be looking for us in the middle of the Sonoran Desert."

Joanna thought about taking a shower and washing off the sweat. "Let's do it. How many hours to Puerto Vallarta after Hermosillo?"

"Sixteen. We get out of the hotel early tomorrow; we'll be at my place before midnight."

They arrived in Hermosillo as the day shifted into night. Heading down a main thoroughfare, Tony pointed out a cluster of hotels.

"Let's try Hotel San Sebastian," said Joanna. "Looks pretty."

They pulled into a promenade that led to the front of the building, which featured a large façade with a giant archway, beyond which lay the hotel. Tony found parking, and they got out, bags in hand.

In the lobby, they checked in with their assumed identities and headed to a room overlooking the pool.

Joanna glanced out the window to see swimmers splashing in the water. Tony walked up behind her. "We could go for a night swim," he said. The feel of Tony behind Joanna made her heart speed up. Then an image of Elliot flashed through her mind, and she felt a wave of guilt. He'd probably been calling her.

"Quarter for your thoughts," said Tony, his breath warming the side of her face. "What are you thinking about?"

"About all the people who must be worried about me right now."

Joanna felt Tony stiffen behind her. Then he backed away and picked up the room service menu. "We better order something if we want to eat tonight. They close up shop pretty early here."

They ate their pizza in silence, Joanna seemingly deep in thought. Maybe this morning in the safe room was an aberration? Tony thought. But here she was, with him, in Mexico.

Tony stood and announced, "Okay if I go shower? Or did you want to go first?"

"Go ahead. I'll let my food digest. But you should cover that wound."

Joanna stood up and looked in a cupboard, locating a trash bag. She waited as Tony removed his shirt, reaching out to help him ease it up over the bandage. She peered inside it. "Looks good. Not too red. But you might want to change it soon." Tony nodded in agreement as she gently tied the plastic bag on his arm, then eyed her handiwork.

"That should do it."

Tony sought her eyes with his, but she averted them, turning to grab the television's remote control instead. As the sound of Spanish filled the room, he picked up his duffel bag, went into the bathroom, and shut the door. For a moment, he stood with his hands on the sides of the sink, trying to swallow the lump of regret lodged in his throat.

When Tony got out of the shower a few minutes later, he found Joanna curled up on the right side of the bed, a slight smile on her lips. He watched the rise and fall of her steady breathing. What was she dreaming about? He wanted to reach out and stroke her hair like he used to when she was asleep.

Taking a blanket out of the closet and a pillow off the bed, he threw them on the couch, then went over and checked the temperature on the air-conditioning unit. Joanna liked it on the warmer side, but he always wanted it cold. How much time had they wasted arguing about nonsense like that? He turned the dial up a notch and laid down on the couch, not bothering with the blanket. Usually, Tony could sleep anywhere, but tonight he had a hard time falling asleep. Instead, he stared at the ceiling, listening to the AC whir and remembering a night several years before.

"You home?"

"In the bedroom!"

Tony pulled off his jacket and set his holster and gun on the dining room table. He walked into their room to find Joanna lounging on the bed in a purple negligee. She had a champagne bucket on the bedside table. The vision of her made him warm all over.

"I'm not complaining, but this isn't usually the way you greet me when

I'm late." Tony walked to the bed and took the glass of champagne Joanna handed him.

"I went to the gynecologist today. He says there's no reason I can't conceive. We just have to keep trying."

Relief flooded Tony. "That's great, Jo. That does call for a toast." Tony lifted his glass and took a swallow.

"I'm ovulating right now."

"Like, right now?"

"Yes, so drink up, take off your clothes, and have your way with me— and hopefully impregnate me."

Tony set down the glass and quickly undressed, then hesitated. "Is there something I'm supposed to do or not do?"

Joanna laughed. "You can do whatever you want. Seriously, Tony, get to it."

15

"You didn't have to sleep on the couch," Joanna said the next morning.

Tony had awoken at dawn and had been watching her sleep from his vantage point. "I didn't want to cramp your style."

Something in Tony's voice alerted Joanna. "You okay? You're not feeling feverish, are you?" She slid out of bed and went over to him, putting her hand on his forehead. "You feel okay. What's up? Is it the pain?"

"No, Jo, I'm fine. The wound is healing nicely. We should probably get on the road."

"Not until you tell me what's wrong. You get some intel I should know about?"

"No, nothing like that."

"Then what is it?"

Tony pushed himself up to a sitting position. "What are we doing?"

Joanna sat down where Tony's legs had been. "We're going to figure out how to shut down the pharma operation. That's what. Seriously, Tony, you okay?"

"I'm talking about us. This. You and me here. And don't tell me there is no us. If I hear that one more time, I can't promise I won't go ballistic."

"What do you want me to say, Tony?" Joanna motioned to stand up, but Tony grabbed her arm and pulled her back down.

"Look me in the eye and tell me you don't love me anymore."

"Tony, please, don't do this." Joanna felt tears push at the back of her eyes, but she would be damned if she let them flow.

Just as quickly as he had grabbed her, he let go of her arm. "Forget I asked. I know where you stand. And I have to accept it." He got up from the couch and began throwing his things in his bag while Joanna watched.

"I thought you needed to take a shower?" he said, finally.

She got up and went into the bathroom, shutting the door behind her and sitting down on the toilet seat while the tears covered her face.

Once on the road again, they made good time. They took turns driving, stopping twice for gas and snacks. Though they talked on the drive, the easy rapport from the day before had vanished.

"Tell me more about your cabin in Puerto Vallarta. You said you have neighbors?" Joanna said at one point when the silence felt like it was closing in on her.

"Yeah, Heriberto and his son, Cortez. Heriberto is a tour guide for a local bus company. The waterfalls in that area are famous, so a lot of people come to see them. They're incredible."

"Does Heriberto have a wife?"

"He did. She died a few years before I moved in. Too bad, too. She sounds like she was a really nice lady."

"That's it? They're your only neighbors?"

"Yep."

"Do you know people in town?"

"You mean are there any women I know?" Tony took his eyes off the road and looked at Joanna. "Why the interest? I'd think you'd be relieved if there was someone. Keep me out of your hair and all."

"I didn't mean that," Joanna sputtered. "I was just wondering about the community you've built there, that's all."

Tony refused to give her the satisfaction of knowing that there was no one in Puerto Vallarta but Heriberto and Cortez. Sure, he knew people in the village, but they were acquaintances, unless you counted Rosalinda, the old lady who ran the bread shop known as a *panaderia*. On a few occasions, Tony had confided in her about Joanna. She was easy to talk to and her churros were delicious.

He felt Joanna waiting for his answer, and he purposefully drew it out. Finally, he spoke. "My community, as you call it, does include some special people. Maybe I'll introduce you to them when we're there. Like Rosalinda, who runs the local bakery."

Tony forced himself not to smirk when he saw Joanna's spine straighten at the mention of Rosalinda. "That would be lovely to meet her and all of your friends," she said. A few minutes later, she closed her eyes, as if to sleep. Good, he thought. It was juvenile, but somehow her wondering about Rosalinda made him feel better.

"So, what's Joanna like? Tell me all about her," said Jesse. They were meeting after work for a drink. For once, Jesse wasn't in the middle of a story and Tony didn't have a case.

"She's gorgeous." Tony said, setting down his beer.

"That's always good," said Jesse. "What else. What does she do?"

"You're never going to believe this, but she's an FBI agent. She just started last year, but she's the real deal."

"Wow, you're right. I didn't expect that, but I guess it makes sense, given the circles you run in. So, things are going well? You have a lot of common interests, besides hunting down bad guys?"

Tony laughed. "Besides laying around all weekend in bed, yeah, there are a lot of common interests. Turns out we're both pretty good at

Backgammon. And we like to cook together. She's Mexican-American, so with her it's a lot of her mama's recipes, like tamales. And then I add my mama's Italian recipes."

"That sounds like fun. I remember the dating days." Jesse sounded wistful.

"You trying to warn me against marriage? I thought you and Clare were happy?"

"We're totally happy. Things just change when you get married. There are responsibilities, like bills, and then when you have kids, that's a whole other thing."

"Is Clare pregnant?"

"Not yet, but we've been talking about it. There's a lot to consider."

"Like what?"

"Like do we want to bring a kid into this world, for one. With my work, and I know with your work, we see the dregs. But I know that Clare will make a wonderful mother. How about Joanna? Have you gotten to the talk about kids someday, or is it still too early?"

"We did talk about it the other day, as a matter of fact."

Jesse laughed. "Then it is serious. What did she say?"

"She wants kids."

"Do you?"

"If she does," said Tony.

"You don't sound too committed, but that's okay, things change. You'll see."

By the time they arrived at the winding, unpaved road that led to the cabin, it was nearly midnight.

"It's really dark out here," commented Joanna as the minivan's lights slit the inky darkness. "How long until your cabin?"

"It's actually not too far from here, but I have to go slow. A lot of wildlife comes out at night."

That was something Joanna hadn't considered. "Like?"

"Deer, wild boar, skunks, coyotes."

"Walking around at night?"

Tony laughed. "Yes, and sometimes running. What did you think they'd be doing?"

Joanna peered out her side window into the night and shifted in her seat uncomfortably.

"You'll be okay. As long as the gang that stormed my house left the door on, that is."

"You might not have a door?"

"Relax. I'm sure if they did take it off the hinges that Heriberto put it back on. I told him that if I ever disappeared or something happened to me to watch over things. And if I was gone for more than a month, to call you with some instructions."

"Me?"

Tony slowed to a crawl, waiting to see what a deer on the side of the road would do. Once it looked like she was going to stay put, he passed the animal. "Yeah, you. Who else would I have him call? My mom isn't getting around too good these days, so I doubt she could make it out here to get my important stuff."

"I didn't know you had important stuff. I never knew you to save much."

"I don't, but there are some things that are important to me."

"Like what?"

"My dad's Purple Heart, for one. My mom gave it to me when I turned eighteen."

This was something Joanna didn't know that Tony had, and it was so important.

"You're quiet."

"I had no idea you had your dad's medal. Why didn't you tell me?"

Tony shrugged. "It never came up. You would have found out, anyway."

"Yeah, when you were dead or missing."

Tony let out a big sigh. "Forget I mentioned it. I'll give it to Jesse or something."

"No, that's okay. I want it. I mean—. If something were to happen to you, it'd be an honor to have it."

"I don't know how your dentist friend would feel about that." Tony braked the car as the cabin came into focus in the car's headlights. "Say hello to my secret hideaway."

16

"I'll go in first and make sure all is clear," said Tony.

Joanna threw up her hands. As she watched Tony head for his house using the light of his cellphone, she remembered her mother's words of advice when she married Tony eighteen years before.

"A man wants to be a man, *hija. Siempre recuerdas.*" Don't take that away from him."

Joanna thought at the time how old school the advice sounded. Now, with Tony insisting on protecting her at every turn, she wondered about those words. Had that been one of their problems? Had she been too self-sufficient?

When Tony indicated all was safe, Joanna gathered her bag and stepped into the night. It was a deep quiet. She didn't think she'd ever experienced such a stillness. Or such bright stars. She looked up at the giant night sky.

"Incredible, isn't it?" Tony had walked up beside her. "There are shooting stars during dry season, which is now."

"I've never seen a shooting star."

"You will. Let me show you the house."

"I see the door is still on," commented Joanna as they walked into the cabin. It was dark, except for the moonlight streaming through the skylight in the center of the room.

Tony turned on a hurricane lamp and held it up, illuminating the space. "The lights seem to be off—I'll have to see what's up with my batteries tomorrow. For tonight, we'll make our way with lanterns. He moved the lamp around so Joanna could see a great room with a couch and table. "It's a pretty simple setup. Here's the living room and my office." On an elevated platform in the center of the room sat a computer desk and what looked like satellite equipment.

"The kitchen faces east, so there's good morning sun there." Tony walked towards the back of the cabin, shining the light on a small kitchen with a bay window. "I even have a garden in the side yard."

Joanna laughed. "A garden? You?"

Tony patted his stomach. "Yeah, I've gotten pretty healthy living off the land here. Heriberto brings me rabbit that he catches, and fish."

"I'm impressed."

"The bedroom and bathroom are in back."

Joanna followed, her pulse quickening at the thought of seeing Tony's bedroom.

It was a small room with a king-sized bed taking up much of the space. No closet, but Tony had a large wooden dresser and matching chest and a small side table on the left side of the bed. He handed her the lantern.

"You can go ahead and wash up. The water won't be warm, but it's never all that cold here. There's some drinking water in the fridge. Tomorrow, I'll send Cortez to town for food and supplies. I'll sleep on the couch."

Joanna reached out her arm and stopped him. "You don't have to sleep on the couch. I can. Your arm will heal better with some good sleep."

"No, Jo, I couldn't. Make yourself at home." Tony walked out of the room and closed the door.

Joanna shined the light around the room. The thought of Tony living in this place for the last three years without her ignited an unidentified emotion. But then, he probably wasn't always alone. What women had been here in her place? Unable to curb the agent in herself, she went to the bedside table and slid the drawer open. Shining the lamp into its contents, she saw two pairs of reading glasses, a book about the planets, and something that made her heart jump into her throat. Reaching in, she picked up a photo. It was her and Tony a few years after they'd married. She had her arms wrapped around him and was gazing up at his face as he grinned into the camera. Gingerly, she placed the photo back in the drawer and slid it shut.

When Joanna awoke in the morning, she found Tony working on some wires in his office. In the light of day, she noted dirty boot marks across the bamboo flooring. Remnants of when they had stormed the cabin.

"Hey, Jo," he said, not looking up. "How'd you sleep? I'm in the middle of some tricky work here, so give me a minute."

She walked up and looked at the gadgetry he was working on. "I'd say I could help you, but you know that would be a lie. I slept good. And you?"

"Just being back here lulled me into dreamland."

Joanna looked out the giant windows Tony had built into the sides of the building at the lush vegetation beyond. Just then, a bird with a yellow belly flew by, landing in a nearby shrub. "What a gorgeous bird!"

"Yellow with a black head? That's my resident kiskadee."

Joanna glanced back at Tony, his head still over his electronics, and felt a wave of envy. Seeing everything he'd been experiencing here made her feel left out.

"Bingo," he said, picking up his phone and listening. "Dial tone. I'm going to call Hammerstein." Joanna watched as he dialed a number and waited.

"Yeah, I know. Twice in two days." Tony laughed. "Look, there's word of a mole in the San Diego FBI office. Can you check it out? Thanks, man."

Tony hung up the phone. "What? I can tell by the look on your face you didn't like something I said."

"You sure you can trust him?"

"He's golden. We've saved each other's asses many times. He was originally LAPD. Why?" Tony walked up to Joanna and studied her closely. "Is there something you're not telling me?"

"That'd be a switch. Me hiding something from you. No, Tony. These are the people I work with we're talking about. I just want to make sure he's legitimate."

"Scout's honor."

Joanna laughed. "Like you were ever a Boy Scout."

Tony gave her a mock expression of hurt.

"What are you going to make us for breakfast, Boy Scout?"

"Let's pick some fruit, then see if Heriberto has any eggs."

"If I'd known improving your diet meant moving out into the jungle, I would have suggested you do this years ago."

Tony laughed and walked out the front door and Joanna followed. Out in the muggy air, Tony headed toward a row of shrubs with a vine intertwined boasting gorgeous purple and white flowers.

"This is passion fruit—these dark purple globes," said Tony, pulling one off the vine.

"Do you just bite into them?" Joanna said, examining its smooth, hard exterior.

"No, I'll show you," Tony said, appearing genuinely enthusiastic to share his world with her. Back inside, he cut the hard shell in half and handed it to Joanna with a spoon, following suit himself.

She spooned out the amber interior filled with juicy pulp and small black seeds and took a tentative taste. "My god, this tastes amazing."

Tony's phone rang just then, and he went to his office to answer. "Yeah?" He listened for a moment, then frowned and asked, "You sure? Okay, thanks."

Joanna watched as Tony set down his phone, a grave look on his face. "What is it?"

"No easy way to say this, Jo. Word is that you're the mole."

17

Joanna felt the color draining from her face. "Tell me you're joking."

Tony stepped down from his office area. "I'm not."

Joanna's hands began to shake. "But my car was bombed! For Christ's sake, that should point to someone else."

"They think you rigged the car to divert attention away from yourself."

"Oh, my god, Tony." She rubbed her hands together to stop them from shaking. "The agency is my life. What am I going to do?"

Joanna searched Tony's face as he took her in his arms. "We'll figure this out. Find out who is framing you and go from there."

Joanna nodded, fighting back tears. She had forgotten how encouraging Tony's embrace could be as he pressed his body into hers. Once she had finally stopped shaking and kept most of the tears at bay, Joanna pulled back and looked into Tony's eyes.

"I know I haven't said it enough. Thank you."

Tony smiled and stroked her hair. "Let's get over to Heriberto's and find out what happened when they stormed my house."

On the way to his neighbor's, Tony wondered if Joanna being framed had something to do with the 14K. He decided to keep his thoughts to himself. Being framed was enough bad news for now. At least they had each other to get to the bottom of things.

"It's okay, Jo. I'll make you some chamomile tea at home like you like."

"I really thought that this time—" Joanna stopped outside the doctor's office, and Tony's heart wrenched when her face crumpled, and tears slid down her cheeks.

"Ah, baby, it'll be okay. We'll keep trying. We'll get this."

"We're out of money. Your money, and from your mom. It's all gone."

"It's just money. I can make more. I'll take some extra shifts."

"I'm sorry." She wiped her tears away with the back of her hand.

Tony took her face in his hands. "Don't apologize for this. We're in this together." He took her in his arms and held her until he felt her stop crying. Then he took the bottom of his shirt and wiped the tears from her eyes.

She gave him a tentative smile. "How about pizza? Those stupid hormones they have me taking make me crave carbs."

"Whatever you want, Jo."

When they arrived at Heriberto's, he was picking guavas. He set the basket down on the ground when he saw Tony approaching.

"*Señor* Tony!" He came running toward them, arms outstretched. "I was so worried about you."

The two men embraced, then Heriberto smiled at Joanna expectantly.

"This is Joanna, Heriberto. My ex-wife."

Heriberto's eyes shone as he looked from one to the other. He extended his hand to Joanna. "*Mucho gusto.* It is a pleasure to have you visit my home. May I offer you some guava juice?"

"*Mucho gusto*, Heriberto. Tony has told me many good things about you. And the juice sounds heavenly. Maybe for our breakfast?"

"We've come to see if you have any fresh eggs," said Tony. "Maybe Cortez can make a run to town when he has a chance and get us some supplies. I'm also hoping you can tell me what happened after I left?"

Heriberto glanced at Joanna.

"It's okay. She knows all about everything."

Heriberto nodded. "Come, let us sit in the outdoor chairs Tony made us. What do you call them again?"

"Adirondacks," said Tony.

Heriberto led them to an area at the back of the house with a firepit and three chairs, each painted a different color. Tony had worked on each one for days. He sat in the red chair and Joanna in the green. Heriberto lowered himself into the yellow chair.

"The night they invaded your home," Heriberto started, "Cortez and I were sitting out here enjoying the night sky. We heard a truck come, so knew that something was wrong, and did as you instructed. We turned off all lights and extinguished our campfire."

"How long were they there?"

"Five, ten minutes. Then they drove away as fast as they came."

"Then what?" asked Tony.

"We didn't approach the cabin until morning, when we were sure they were gone. The door was open, and there were many things upside down. We did our best to clean up. There were wires pulled from your satellite and solar systems."

"Well, I appreciate you looking after things."

"That's what neighbors are for. Now let me get you some eggs from *las gallinas.*"

"He seems like a very sweet man." Joanna said after he walked off to the chicken coop to gather eggs.

"He's good people. Really helped me when I first moved in here. And obviously still is."

"So, they didn't get the intel?" Joanna whispered when Heriberto was out of earshot.

"No, I've got it hidden well."

"Are you going to show me the intel?"

"Of course. We need to scour it for clues. Like what the connection to your office is, and who's in charge of the pharma ring."

"You think the FBI mole has something to do with your case?"

"I'm starting to. How many people work in the San Diego head-quarters?"

"About twenty-five, twelve of them active agents. And my boss."

"What do you know about her?"

"Sumner? She's as straight as they come. She graduated top of her class at Quantico. A legend for her sharpshooting. I can't imagine her being a mole. She has so much to lose."

"Sometimes those with the most to lose risk the most. What about your partner, Rodriguez?"

Joanna didn't answer at first. "He once had some gambling issues. He'd go to Reno and wouldn't show up for work. But he got help a couple of years ago. He's been steady ever since."

Tony thought for a moment. "Being in debt to loan sharks is a whole lot of motive."

"I can't imagine that Rodriguez would throw his career away over gambling debt." Joanna shook her head. "Although he did almost lose his marriage over it, so I guess it's possible. The thought makes my head reel, but at this point, I have to admit he's our best suspect."

18

On the way back to Tony's, Joanna thought more about Rodriguez. Over the last few months, her partner had been less talkative than usual. The thought made her feel uneasy.

"You're quiet," said Tony.

The air buzzed with insects, and she felt sweat forming on her brow. Suddenly, something shrieked in the trees above, and she jumped. "What was that?"

"A macaw. Beautiful birds. The ones here aren't as colorful as in some areas of the world, but the lime green is cool."

Joanna smiled and cocked her head.

"What?" Tony tugged on some foliage hanging from a tree above them.

"This is a new side of you."

"What side is that?"

"The Daniel Boone side. I never knew you to be so tuned in to nature."

"Well, there isn't all that much to do out here, if you hadn't noticed. Truth is, I've always liked nature. I used to play in the woods near my home in Jersey when I was young. Then when we moved to San Diego, I made the orange groves my second home. I guess you could call it getting back to my roots."

"It looks good on you."

Tony grinned. "Yeah? How good?" He walked toward her.

Joanna stepped back without thinking, then felt like kicking herself when she saw a flash of disappointment cross Tony's face.

"Let's get back so we can cook up these eggs," he said, turning and marching forward.

Back in the kitchen, Tony scrambled up the eggs and handed her the plate, garnished with slices of mango.

"I can see what you mean about healthy eating," she said to break the silence. She sat down on a stool at a small table that appeared to be made from a tree trunk. "Is this what I think it is?" she asked, admiring the multiple rings.

"I cut it off a tree that fell in a storm last year. Gorgeous, huh?" Tony sat down and ran his hands along the smooth surface. "I sanded this thing for hours."

"It's gorgeous. Everything here is lovely." Joanna looked up to see a faraway look on Tony's face. Was he thinking of how she had pulled away from him? Why had she done that when what she really wanted to do was walk toward him?

When they finished eating, Tony took their dishes to the sink. "Let's have a look at the intel."

"Sounds good to me." Joanna stood and stretched.

Tony knelt on the floor by the back wall, pulling up the baseboard to reveal two buttons. He pushed one, and the painting on the wall above slid open, exposing a safe. "That other button opens up the tunnel," he said. "And I have a remote for it, if we need to leave quickly."

He pressed buttons on the safe and it popped open. Extracting a hard drive, he took it over to his office. Once installed in the computer, Joanna brought a chair from the kitchen and sat next to him.

"So, this is where you've been hiding for the last three years," she mused.

"Pretty much." Tony typed in a code and a series of numbers popped up, then words. He scrolled through pages of documentation. "These are reports of people having mysterious symptoms and even dying from the counterfeit drugs."

"That's a lot of people."

"Sadly, yes." He pointed to another screen of photos. "How about we go through these and see what you can come up with."

"Surveillance photos? Where'd you get them?"

"I was able to take some images from satellite. Others I got from contacts. Some were on the internet. I've been trying to piece together the puzzle of who all the players are." Tony opened a chart of connections and Joanna leaned in, amazed at the detail. "Tony, this is incredible. It must have taken you months. We could use this level of intricacy on all our intel at the bureau."

"Not sure I ever thought about working at the FBI, but I'll take that as a compliment," he said. "Right before I left for San Diego, I felt like I was on the verge of figuring out who is in charge. You see this." He pointed to a section with several question marks. "This American guy appears here and there with the 14K. I've got him in photos talking to several members. I think he's involved somehow, but I haven't untangled just how."

Joanna's eyes fixed on the man at the end of Tony's finger. "I swear I've seen that guy before." The man looked about forty, with close-cropped brown hair and a grimace on his face.

Joanna shut her eyes and tried to visualize the circumstances. "It seems like it wasn't that long ago." She could feel Tony waiting patiently, his steady support. "Good grief!" She finally opened her eyes, exasperated. "I can't place him."

"Remember when you used to tell me if you started talking about something else, anything else, it would jog your memory, and your mind would solve the problem in the background?" He put his hand on her upper back and rubbed it gently.

"Okay," said Joanna. "Why don't you tell me about the woman who runs the bakery?"

Tony pulled his hand away and laughed.

"What's so funny? I'm just trying to make conversation. Find out about your life here."

"You want to know about Rosalinda? Not anyone else I might know here. And why is that, Jo?"

"I don't know," she sputtered. "Besides Heriberto and his son, you haven't mentioned anyone else."

"Could it be because she's a woman?"

Joanna felt Tony scrutinizing her reaction. She knew she had talked herself into this corner. "Yes, I'm interested because she's a woman, okay? In fact, I'm not liking my feelings about her. Did you talk to her about us?"

The look on Tony's face said it all.

"What are you doing talking to her about us?"

"You mean to tell me you haven't told your dentist friend about us?"

"No. Yes. I don't know."

"So, it's okay for you to talk about us, but not me?"

Joanna crossed her arms. "You can talk to anyone you want. Go talk to her tonight, if you want to."

"I can't if it's past seven pm." Tony grinned.

"Oh, an early riser?"

"She's been an early riser her whole life. All eighty-seven years of it."

When Tony's comment sunk in, Joanna felt her face heat up. "Rosalinda is an old lady?"

Tony's eyes were laughing.

"Why didn't you—," Joanna started to say, then it hit her. "I know where I saw that man!"

"Where?"

"At a districtwide conference for agents. He's FBI."

19

"Does he work in your office?"

"No, the LA office."

"Can you identify his photo in an FBI database?"

"My clearance doesn't go that high." Joanna struggled to recall that night more clearly.

"I see your wheels turning." Tony stood up. "Let's take a walk. It'll clear our heads."

Joanna shrugged as they walked out into the midday sun. Tony headed for the cool coverage of the jungle. When they came to a fork in the path, they turned away from the house.

"Where are you taking me?" The foliage was incredibly green and lush, the scent of humus in the air. At one point, Joanna heard water falling in the distance. The more they walked, the louder the water sounded.

"It's a surprise." Tony continued at a fast clip. She rushed after him, nearly tripping on vines in her path. "Jeez, Tony, give me a chance to catch up."

"We're just about there," he yelled back. "Don't be a wussy."

Joanna had always hated it when he called her that. The irritation made her move faster, until she was on his heels.

They came to an embankment where into a pool of water, a giant waterfall cascaded down the side of a mountain. It reached at least five-hundred feet, its force deafening. Tiny droplets of water cooled her skin.

"This is one of my favorite spots," Tony shouted over the sound of the water. "I come here to think."

"Only you could think with this ruckus going on," Joanna cried.

They stood side-by-side for a time watching the water show. Something about the ferocity of the water as it crashed its way down and pounded on the surface of the pool gave her courage. Joanna reached over and slid her hand into Tony's warm one. She felt him turn to look at her, but she kept staring straight ahead, her insides as chaotic as the waterfall.

After a few more minutes in silence, they headed back. When they arrived at Tony's house, they found Heriberto and his son waiting for them.

"You must be Cortez," Joanna said to the gangly boy, whose brown eyes lit up his face when he smiled.

He nodded and extended his hand to shake hers.

"Can I get you guys something to drink?" Tony asked them.

"No, we won't stay long. Cortez remembered something to tell you. We also brought groceries."

Tony turned to Cortez and waited for the boy to speak.

"Two days after you left," he said shyly, "I came to check your cabin. I saw a man and a woman here. They had a car. A red one. Maybe a Toyota."

"What were they doing?"

"I saw them inside, and then they got back in the car and drove away. I haven't seen them again."

"If I showed you a photo, could you identify the man?"

"I will try."

Tony walked them all into his cabin and turned on his computer. He pulled up the photo of the unidentified FBI agent.

"That's him," said Cortez, stuffing his hands in his jeans pockets.

"That helps me more than you know, Cortez. Thank you." Tony turned to Heriberto and handed him some cash for the groceries. Then he moved to give Cortez money, but the boy protested. "No, *Señor* Tony, we are just being good neighbors."

"Didn't you say you wanted to buy your friend Maria something for her birthday?"

The boy's face colored a deep red.

"Buy her something nice." Tony pressed what looked like twenty pesos into his hand. The boy grinned and slid the bill into his pocket.

After he got off the phone a few minutes later, Tony appeared pleased. "His name is Reginald Stewart. And he's recently come into some big money. At one point, the Bureau investigated some of his larger purchases, but someone has his back. Every time the heat gets turned up on this guy, it quickly gets turned off. He's currently in L.A."

"Where are the pharmaceuticals being distributed?"

"All over Southern California. Quite a few pediatric clinics specializing in asthma and allergies."

"Do you know the distribution route?"

"From Hong Kong, Taiwan or China to LAX, and from there a bunch of mules come and cart the drugs to the doctors' offices. Not your typical mules, though. They're dressed like pharmaceutical reps. What I'm not clear on is if the doctor's offices know they're counterfeit drugs."

Joanna strummed her fingers on the desk. "Maybe not. If patients don't get better or die, that doesn't do the doctor any good."

Tony brought the documents up on the screen again and they continued to study them for several more hours, but nothing emerged. He finally stretched his arms overhead. "How about we call this a day? Want a beer?"

As much as Joanna wanted to figure this all out tonight, they'd be better off tackling more in the morning.

"A beer sounds great." She walked up behind him to peer into the refrigerator. "Wow, thank you, Heriberto."

"I could shop on my own, but a couple months of my pension from the

LAPD is more than Heriberto makes in a year. Him shopping for me gives me a chance to give him some extra cash."

"That's nice of you." Joanna took one of the beers Tony pulled out of the fridge. He also removed a round of soft Mexican cheese. Picking up a box of multigrain crackers from the counter and a wooden cutting board, he brought it all outside.

Tony turned off the lights in the house behind him and shut the door, washing the front porch in twinkling starlight.

"I need to conserve the solar, plus you can see the stars better." He sat down in the chair next to her and took a long pull of his beer, then pointed to the sky. "This is my television. I've actually gotten good at identifying the constellations."

"I want to see a shooting star."

"You will."

They sat and listened to the sound of insects humming in the nearby jungle as they munched on cheese and crackers and drank their beers. Joanna was beginning to wonder if Tony was exaggerating when she saw a flash of light plummet from the sky.

She gasped. "I think that was a shooting star?"

"Hurry, wish," Tony said.

Joanna shut her eyes and scrambled for something to wish for, settling on getting her name cleared with the FBI.

"Well?"

"Well, what?" she asked.

"What'd you wish for?"

"That will jinx it," she said.

"That's just with birthday candles. Tell me."

"I wished that we would expose the real mole and clear my name. What about you?"

Tony was quiet for a moment. Finally, he said, "The same thing I've wished for every single time I've seen a shooting star. This."

"This?"

"You and me here, together, talking."

20

Tony waited for Joanna's response. When she didn't say a word, he finished drinking his beer and stood up. "I'm going inside to cook us up some dinner."

In the kitchen, he cut up some chicken and vegetables for a stir fry. As he watched the food cook, his mind ran through various scenarios involving Reginald Stewart and Rodriguez. He had always hated this point in a case when he was a detective. So close but with none of the pieces fully fitting together.

"Smells wonderful," said Joanna. "You look deep in thought."

"Just thinking about the case. Bad habit. I have a hard time turning it off."

"I'm the same way. My head is still trying to wrap around the possibility of Rodriguez being a mole. I went to his wedding."

"Well, we don't know for sure. Tomorrow, we can do a deep dive into his finances."

While Tony got ready for bed, Joanna went outside again to admire the sky. She found what she thought was the big dipper and waited for another shooting star, but one never came. After a while, she went back inside to get some sleep. When she passed Tony sleeping, his long frame awkwardly stretched out on the couch, she felt a pang of guilt.

A few minutes later, she slid between the sheets in his room and soon found herself drifting off, but it wasn't easy slumber. She tossed and turned, repeatedly waking from nightmares about losing her job and even being tried for treason. About three in the morning, she woke up struggling to breathe.

She looked at the side of the bed where Tony always slept, thinking how he used to stroke her hair when she couldn't sleep. Now here she lay so close and yet so far from him. Sliding out of bed, she padded into the living room, where the moonlight bathed everything in silver light. She walked up silently to Tony, watching him sleep. He suddenly bolted upright, extracting a gun from the couch cushions.

"Tony," she said.

"Shit, sorry." He put down the gun. "Warn me or something next time. What's the matter?"

Joanna tried to force the lump in her throat back down. "Outside earlier. Did you mean what you said about us and shooting stars?"

Tony didn't say anything, but he nodded, his eyes searching her face.

"Come sleep with me?" Joanna's voice was almost a whisper.

"Bad dreams?"

She took his hand, and they headed to the bedroom, settling beneath the sheets. "Yes." She cuddled up next to his body and embraced him.

Tony began caressing her hair, and Joanna felt her body relax. How good it was to have him near her, with her. It felt so easy and natural.

"You'll sleep soon, baby." He soothed her, his words low and comforting.

"What if I don't want to sleep?" she said softly.

Turning around and looking into Tony's eyes, Joanna asked, "What if I asked you to make love to me?"

Tony frowned. "Look, Jo, I'm not sure what you really want."

"I've missed you, Tony. All I want right now is to be with you."

Tony's heart happily flip-flopped in his chest, and he pulled her to him, his lips hungrily seeking hers. She responded by welcoming him with her mouth, then pulled her lips free. Then she reached down and took him in her hand and began stroking. "Let's take this slow," she said, feeling herself swell.

"Whatever you want, Jo. I'll stay here all night like this."

She stroked him more quickly, and he groaned. He reached for her, but she pulled away.

"You don't want me to touch you?" he said.

"Shh. I'm taking care of you right now." She ran her tongue down the center of his chest, making her way below.

"Okay," he breathed.

She kissed him with her mouth and ran her tongue around the outside of his penis, which seemed to send a lightning bolt through him. He panted, "Baby, I'm not sure how much more of this I can take."

Joanna placed her finger lightly on his lips. Then she moved on top of him, guiding him in. She rocked her hips back and forth, keeping her eyes locked on his. She could tell he was holding himself until she was satisfied. She began pumping harder on him, her body urging his to let go. When he did, her own body succumbed to the sweeping desire, and they both cried out simultaneously. She lay on top of him for a while as their heartbeats settled, then shifted into a steady rhythm together.

"I've missed you so much, Tony. Please don't ever leave me again," said Joanna. When Tony didn't reply, she heard his steady breathing. She stayed put, so as not to break the spell.

Tony woke the next morning to the distant sound of Heriberto's chickens squawking as they laid their eggs. He felt Joanna's breathing beside him and smiled.

"Tony, is that you? I'm back here."

He had just gotten off a sixteen-hour stakeout and was glad to be home. He walked down the hall to find her standing in the doorway of the bathroom, a white stick in her hand, eyes gleaming.

"Is that what I think it is?" He approached carefully, as if the white plastic instrument was fragile.

When they came face-to-face, Joanna stuck out the pregnancy test so he could see. "Plus sign, Tony."

He nodded, not trusting himself to speak. Finally, he managed to say, "Does that mean what I think it means?"

"The in-vitro worked. We're going to have a baby!" She began jumping up and down, and he reached out for her. "Whoa, maybe you shouldn't be doing that?"

Joanna stopped jumping and frowned. "Aren't you happy about this?"

"I'm thrilled. I just want to make sure you're okay, that's all."

"I'm perfect now, Tony. Absolutely perfect."

21

When Joanna finally stirred, Tony kissed the top of her head. "Hey, sleepyhead."

"Good morning," she murmured, opening her eyes.

"Sleep good?"

She nodded her head against his side.

"No regrets, I hope."

"Not at all. I was just thinking about how it's time to get back to reality, though."

"We better get working. Truth is, I don't know how much longer we can stay here safely. The 14K did storm the place, so it's not farfetched to think the FBI could do the same."

Joanna sat up, and Tony admired her bare breasts and black hair spilling down her back. "I've missed this," he said.

She smiled. "Me, too."

An hour later, Tony pushed his chair back from the desk and stretched his neck.

"Anything?"

"Nothing. I see where Rodriguez was having financial trouble a few years ago like you mentioned. A bunch of charges at a casino in Reno, and some big cash withdrawals. But that came from a home equity line of credit he took out. Then that stopped completely around the time you said he started going to gambling support groups. The most he has spent since then was dinner out and some big appliances. A refrigerator and stove. No cash deposits."

"Any signs of offshore bank accounts?"

"*Nada*. From where I sit, he's clean."

Joanna let out a breath. "That makes me feel better. I know it doesn't get us any closer to finding the mole, but the thought of Rodriguez betraying me…" she trailed off.

"You find anything?" he asked her.

"I may have. I want you to look at some footage. A drugstore in San Diego. One of the drug mules impersonating a pharmaceutical sales rep. Something looks off." Joanna pressed a button on her laptop and a surveillance tape showed the front of the drugstore as a black sedan pulled up. Two Asian women got out of the car and headed inside.

"Back that up to where the taller woman is closing the car door," said Tony. "Focus in on her hand." Joanna zoomed in and froze the frame. Her hand had what appeared to be a tattoo featuring five dots in the shape of a Y.

"I'll be damned," said Tony. "I think we found our leader. And I've been looking for a man this whole time. See that tattoo. Tattoos aren't as common among the Asian gangs as other gangs, but that's a symbol for the Asian Triads."

"Twitch said the leader spoke Chinese but had a high-pitched voice. Maybe what was strange was the fact she's a woman, not a man," said Joanna.

"Exactly. And I wonder who the other female is? There's a shot of her face. Let's see if Hammerstein can run her photo through facial recognition." He captured an image, then emailed it to him.

Joanna's head ached from needing to eat, but she didn't want to stop. She glanced up from the computer screen when Tony said, "I think I got something. A meet tomorrow."

"You're kidding. How did you discover that?"

"I found a name in my intel from six months ago. I almost missed it. Not an Asian name, though. Samantha Smothers. I heard recently that the 14K has been using social media to communicate with members. So, I put her name into the LinkedIn search engine and looked at her messaging. They're talking about meeting down south of the border tomorrow."

"Time to pack?"

"Let's eat first."

Tony plopped leftovers into a pot and put a flame under it. Joanna got out a spoon and reached across him to have a taste.

"Hey, you born in a cave?" He grinned. "Let me put some on a plate for you."

"Why dirty up dishes? I don't mind eating out of the pan. Sometimes it tastes better that way." She dipped her spoon in for more and turned to face him. Joanna leaned in close, the spoon aimed at his mouth, her thigh pressed warm against his.

"You feeding me now?"

"You complaining?" she said.

"Nah, go ahead." He closed his eyes and opened his mouth. Joanna put a spoonful of food in his mouth. Keeping his eyes closed, he cleaned off the spoon, chewed, and swallowed. "You're right. It does taste better," he opened his eyes, "but I'm thinking it might be the delivery system." He reached around and grabbed her bottom with both hands, pulling her closer.

Joanna laughed. "How am I going to feed you, if you're holding my ass?"

Tony grinned. "You'll manage."

"How about you show me?"

He hiked up her skirt and ran his hand up along her thigh.

Joanna's breath caught, and she giggled. She refilled the spoon. "Chew," she said, suddenly stern. She watched as he chewed and swallowed.

His dark brown eyes looked at her so intently, she blushed and looked away. He took the bottom of her tank top and began to lift it. Joanna didn't object, instead raised both arms over her head in order to help him.

"I'm ready for dessert," he said, his voice low and husky. Joanna hadn't finished dressing this morning, her breasts bare beneath her shirt, her nipples hard now.

Tony tossed her t-shirt on the counter and stood there quietly, taking in her beauty. She saw his groin strain with desire against his pants and wondered how they had ever let one another go. She reached out and stroked him, the area hot beneath her hand, a breath catching in his throat. He lifted her to the kitchen counter. Pushing her skirt up to her hips and closing his eyes, he began feeling her as if he were sightless, holding her breasts in his hands, tasting them, running his fingers across them, then his mouth sending a hot wave of desire rushing through her. When he was done, he spread her legs and pushing her panties aside, slipped his tongue inside her, moving it deep and slow.

Joanna dug her fingers into his shoulder. "Right here in the kitchen?" she breathed.

"Why not?" he said. "A perfect place to devour you."

"I want to look at the sky through the skylight when you make love to me, Tony."

He lifted her up, and she wrapped her legs about his waist as he carried her to the couch under the skylight. Once there, he eased her onto the sofa. Then, breasts bare, skirt up around her waist, he removed her sandals and rubbed and kissed her toes, then stripped off her panties. Next he began to undress, peeling off his clothes as she watched. He stripped down slowly, displaying his hard body sculpted by living in the jungle and doing so much hard work. Joanna couldn't take her eyes off him. When he couldn't take it anymore, he mounted her, taking it as slow and easy as he could until they both were satisfied. When they finished, Joanna caressed his cheek, searching for the right words to convey what she was feeling. "Tony, there's something I want to tell you," she whispered the words.

Suddenly, there was a sharp rapping on the front door. They both sat upright. Tony hastily pulled on his pants and ran a hand through his hair, while Joanna got dressed. Grabbing his gun, Tony padded barefoot to the front door, pulling it open.

"Cortez, what's up?"

"*Señor* Tony. Some men just came to the house. They have my father!"

22

"*Tranquilo*, Cortez," said Tony. "Tell us everything." Joanna pulled up a chair for the boy to sit down.

"Me and *Papá* were tending the fruit trees," he started, clasping and unclasping his hands rapidly. "I was up high in the mango tree when they came. *Papá* told me to be quiet, then he tried to talk to them. They were asking if there were other houses nearby." Cortez stopped. He looked almost terrified to speak.

"Then what?" asked Tony.

"*Papá* told them he was the only one in this part of the jungle. They said they knew he was a tour guide and wanted him to show them around. When he said he only worked through the tour company, the man took out a gun and made him go with them."

"How many people were there?"

"A man and a woman."

"Cortez, we all need to get out of here right now. We're taking you with us," said Joanna in a low, level voice. "We're going to find your father, but we have to leave before they find us. Let us pack some things, and we'll go."

Joanna and Tony raced to prepare their bags. Within minutes they were ready to leave.

"We're going on an adventure, Cortez," said Tony. He went to the back of the house and pushed a button on a remote control. A door slid open in the wall, causing the boy's eyes to widen. Tony gestured for Cortez and Joanna to head in, then he followed, watching the door slide shut again before turning to them both.

"We need to follow some ground rules. Tunnels can be dangerous. We don't know who or what we'll be running into. Stay together at all times and listen."

Tony directed his attention at Cortez, who nodded. *"Pero, mi papá.* I don't want to leave him." The boy looked distraught.

"We're going to find your father." Tony told him. "And I'm doing what he would want, which is keep you safe. Now let's go. We've got a long road ahead of us." Tony looked at Cortez's feet. "I hope those tennis shoes are comfortable."

"I always use them to climb the trees."

They made their way through the dusty dirt tunnel with Cortez in between Joanna and Tony. As they traveled, the passageway narrowed significantly, and Joanna became more and more uneasy. At one point, she felt her throat tighten and had to stop and lean against the wall to catch her breath. How did Tony stand traveling these tunnels all the way from Puerto Vallarta to San Diego?

Cortez stopped. "You okay, *Señora?*"

"Jo, you alright?" Tony chimed in, coming back to her.

She nodded, then finally spoke. "I'm just not liking how the tunnel keeps getting smaller and smaller."

"It gets bigger when we reach San Juan de Abajo. If we can get out there, I'll call Hammerstein to see what information he can get on the woman we saw on the intel video. But we might have to come into the tunnel again to lie low."

"We're going to sleep in here, *Señor* Tony?"

"If we have to."

Cortez eyed Joanna. "I don't think the *Señora* likes that idea."

"I'll be okay," said Joanna. "And Cortez. My name is Joanna."

They resumed walking, and soon the tunnel began to enlarge. Tony then stopped suddenly and held out his arm.

Joanna heard voices in the distance speaking Spanish.

"Looks like we've got some company," said Tony. "We may need to negotiate our way out. Let me take the lead."

"My Spanish is better than yours," Joanna protested as Tony got out his gun. Cortez appeared petrified.

"Everything is going to be fine," she assured him. "Tony and I are trained for this. Just follow us. If there is any problem, run back into the tunnel."

The voices became louder as they approached. When they sounded a few yards away, Tony stopped. Joanna strained to listen.

"Sounds like thugs planning for a drug run," she whispered. "How do you want to play this?"

"I'll go in first. Something happens, you and Cortez head the other way with the bags."

When Tony rounded the corner, he kept his gun hidden in the back of his pants. In response to the guns drawn on him, he put up his hands. As he did so, he surveyed the scene. Three Mexican wannabe thugs, skittish with their guns.

"*Tranquilo.* I just want to exit here," he said in a level voice.

"What the hell you doing here, *hombre?*" A guy with tattoos on his neck and a red bandana on his head skulked toward him.

Tony looked up at the ladder and manhole above. "Me and my wife and kid are trying to get away from some trouble. You let us out of here with no hassle, I'll make it worth your while."

"You got *dinero, hombre?* The price to *salir* is steep."

"I'll pay what I think is fair. After my *mujer* and *niño* are out."

"Where are they?"

"Right here," announced Joanna, coming around the corner with Cortez and their bags in tow.

"*Hola, guapa,*" said the leader when he saw Joanna. He puffed his chest up and grinned at his friends. "How about you and me talk for a while before we let you out?"

Tony stiffened when he saw Joanna's face morph. He knew that look. It meant, I'll show you who the hell is boss.

"Just let us pass and all's good," Tony reasoned.

"After me and pretty *esposa* have a talk," said the leader as he swaggered towards Joanna. She let him come close, then pushed Cortez back and pulled her gun, aiming it at the guy's face.

"One more step, and I'll shoot. And you won't like where."

The leader put one hand up and seemed to weigh his options. Finally, he ordered his sidekicks to stand down. "*Cálmate, guapa,* we'll let you and your old man and *niño* go. I prefer my women without weapons." He laughed at his own joke.

Joanna didn't flinch. She motioned for Cortez to run to the ladder, keeping her gun trained on the men. When it was Joanna's turn, Tony stood by the ladder with his gun drawn as she climbed up with one bag, then returned for the other.

"This is where we say *adiós,*" said Tony, once Joanna had finished.

"Where's our *dinero,* old man?"

"You pissed me off disrespecting my woman, so you get nothing. You're lucky she didn't shoot your balls off. But I'll give you one thing you can take to your boss."

"Yeah, what's that?"

"The 14K are taking over this tunnel."

The leader laughed. "You *loco, gringo?*"

"No, I'm dead serious."

Then Tony climbed the ladder and surfaced aboveground. "Looks like the tunnels aren't going to be a safe place to call it a night," he said. "Let's find lodging, then figure out our next move."

Cortez glanced from Tony to Joanna. "Is *papá* here in this town?"

Night was falling and lights were turning on in the nearby houses, one by one.

"We're not sure where your father is, but we're going to find him," said Tony.

Joanna nodded in agreement. "Your father is very strong and brave. He's going to be okay while we search for him." She hoped it was true.

23

They found a small hotel in town run by a jovial man named Domingo, who offered them some dinner.

"*Mi esposa* has cooked plenty," he announced, setting his burrito down when they walked into the hotel's lobby, which appeared to be the front room of the cottage in which the family lived. A sign on the desk noted that there were five separate cottages in the back for guests, and two were vacant.

One look at Cortez devouring the burrito with his eyes sold Joanna. She pulled out twenty *pesos* and handed it to him. "Would this cover four burritos?"

"More than enough." He accepted the money humbly. "Let me introduce you to Gabriella, *mi esposa.*"

Joanna followed him behind the counter, stepping through a small doorway into a tiny kitchen. A large woman with generous breasts turned to greet them. She worked on a wooden island in the kitchen assembling burritos, a big pot of beans bubbling on the stove behind her.

"This nice lady would like some burritos, *mi amor,*" said Domingo, his eyes shining when they met his wife's. How long had they been married, wondered Joanna? Their adoring glances reminded her of her own parents.

"*Ah, te ves cansada, pobrecita. Sientate.*" Gabriella waved her to a stool next to the island.

"I am a bit tired, thank you," said Joanna. "Your cooking smells delicious."

The woman smiled and took a large ceramic plate out of a cupboard, piling on the burritos and scoops of extra beans on the side. She then opened a cast-iron oven and extracted a tray of tortilla strips and piled them into an earthenware bowl.

"*Gracias, Señora,*" said Joanna, grateful that at least one problem was solved for the night. They might not be finding Cortez's father just yet, but at least his son would be fed and have a roof over his head. "Let me get my son to help carry this to our room."

Joanna went back to where Tony was chatting with Domingo and got Cortez, who readily followed her into the kitchen.

"Ay, what a *guapo* boy you have," Gabriella said, beaming.

"*Mucho gusto.*" Cortez greeted her, smiling shyly as he took the bowl of chips.

In the room a few minutes later, Joanna set the food on a small table. "Wash your hands first," she instructed Cortez. As he walked away and into the bathroom, she noticed how unfamiliar, yet comforting it felt to have a child with them.

When he was out of earshot in the bathroom, the water running, she spoke. "Any ideas on retrieving Heriberto? And what the hell is going on?"

"They must not be familiar with the area. Otherwise, they wouldn't need a tour guide. That tells me one important thing. They don't know where my house is."

"And Heriberto is so loyal to you, he's not going to tell them."

Cortez had just finished gobbling down two burritos when Tony cleared his throat. "We know you have questions about where your father is. Finding him is our top priority. And I know he would want you to listen to me. Why don't you go take a shower and me and Joanna are going to discuss our next move?" He handed the boy a pair of sweatpants and a t-shirt. "These are going to be big on you."

Cortez nodded, his eyes misting with threatened tears.

When Tony heard the water running in the shower, he pulled out his hard drive. "Can you connect this to your laptop? I want to take another look. There has to be something we missed."

Joanna pulled out her computer and plugged in the hard drive. Within minutes, they were scrolling through surveillance footage again.

Tony's phone buzzed and he pulled it out of his pocket. "Hammerstein." He hit speakerphone.

"Where'd you get that photo you emailed me?"

"Surveillance photos I took a few months ago," Tony replied. "You know who she is?"

"Ju Wang. We've been watching her for months. Her father is Triad, and she's suspected of involvement. Was she with anyone?"

"Another woman, who had the Triad tattoo on her hand."

"That's unheard of for a woman to have a Triad tattoo."

"I know. Trying to wrap my head around this. Does she have any known companions?"

"Yes, Song Do. He's elusive, though. We've suspected him of high-level involvement for a while, but we can't seem to get anything concrete on him, not even a photo. Not sure about the other female you mentioned seen with Wang. By the way, you and your ex are on the FBI's wanted list."

"Great. Hope this doesn't put you in an awkward position."

"I've been in worse."

"Listen, there's another wrinkle in the case. My neighbor, Heriberto, got nabbed yesterday, leaving behind his ten-year-old son. The son said they needed his father as a tour guide. Good news is that once I find him, I'm pretty sure it'll lead me to the head of the pharma operation."

"Higher ups want that stopped pronto," said Hammerstein. "There were more unexplained deaths this past weekend."

"We'll keep digging."

Tony hung up just as Cortez exited the bathroom. His hair was wet, and Tony's clothing looked ten sizes too big. Joanna went to him. "Would you like me to roll up your pant legs?"

When he nodded, Tony watched as Joanna knelt beside the boy and gently rolled up the pants, tying the excess fabric.

"*Gracias*," the boy said softly as tears began to spill down his cheeks.

"Aw, Cortez," said Joanna, pulling him to her. "Keep good thoughts and stay strong, okay?"

Tony's heart ached as he watched the scene. For Cortez and for Joanna, who would have made such a good mother.

Tony and his partner at the LAPD were staking out a massage parlor downtown, waiting for the fleabag they'd been tailing for months to emerge. He looked at Joanna's number coming through. He knew what she wanted. They were supposed to go to her folks' for dinner, but he wasn't going to make it. He was about to hit answer on his cell, when their perp walked out onto the street and headed for a car. Tony hit ignore instead and got ready to follow their target.

His partner shook his head. "Man, if I ignore calls from my wife, I pay for it bigtime later. I let her know I might not be home for days this time."

"Well, Joanna isn't your wife," said Tony. "She works for the FBI. She gets the work. I don't need to tell her."

His partner shrugged his shoulders. "I've learned from experience that it's better to say sorry now than later."

"Look, me and Joanna are solid."

"Before you go to bed, Cortez, how about we ask you some more questions about today and the people who took your father?"

Cortez came to the table, his eyes solemn. "Do you think they are feeding *mi papá, Señor* Tony?"

"I'm sure they are," said Tony. "Like I said, they need him to be their tour guide. Let's think back about the people who took him. You said it was a man and a woman, right?"

Cortez nodded.

"If I show you a photo of the lady, would you recognize her?"

"I think so."

Tony pulled up the photo of Ju Wang.

"Was this the lady?"

Cortez shook his head. "The *señora* had, what do you call it, *pelo rubio*. I think she was American."

"Blonde hair?" Joanna piped in.

He nodded. "And the man had brown hair. He was also American."

Tony pulled out a photo of Reginald Stewart.

"That's him," said Cortez excitedly. "That's the man."

"Great, Cortez. This will really help us find your father. Go try and get some sleep now."

Once he was out of earshot, Tony remarked, "How in the hell did Stewart get on our tail?"

24

"I don't know which is worse," said Tony. "The 14K on our asses, or the FBI informant for them."

"And who is the blonde?" mused Joanna. She got out her computer. "I'm going to gain unauthorized access into Bureau personnel records and check the L.A. and San Diego offices. We find the blonde, we find Stewart, Heriberto, and the Chinese."

Joanna pulled up the FBI payroll files and perused the list. When she came across Sumner's salary, she commented. "Bureau chiefs are getting paid more than I thought nowadays."

Tony got up and stood behind her as she scanned the files. "Shit, better than all the complaints I've heard. More reason for Sumner not to be our snitch. But your assistant Cara is making a paltry sum."

"She's taking classes at Quantico. She'll be getting a pay raise once she graduates."

"I hate to say this, but we need to check out everyone."

"She is blonde, but her father is also career FBI, and a decorated agent. I seriously doubt she'd opt for treason, but I'll check out her finances."

They spent the next two hours investigating the finances of every single female in her office and came up empty-handed.

"No offshore accounts. No big deposits." Tony yawned.

"Let's get some shuteye," Joanna suggested, feeling fatigue settled deeply into her bones and mind. "Start fresh in the morning."

"What do you think of this color for the nursery?" asked Joanna. "Yellow is a pretty neutral color. Or black. On second thought, black is perfect."

"Uh, huh."

Joanna grabbed Tony's arm and shook it. "Why aren't you listening to me?"

"Sorry, Jo, I got the case on my mind. I know I'm supposed to leave it at the door like we agreed, but it's eating at me."

"Put it out of your mind and take a look at these paint swatches, or else you're going to have no say in the color of the baby's room."

"Now that would be tragic," he said, checking out the color tiles on the table. "I like purple," he said, pointing to a paint chip. "It's a royal color, isn't it?"

"Purple if it's a boy? You sure about that?"

"It's not going to be a boy."

"And how do you know that? I'll kill you, Tony, if you asked the doctor the sex. We decided to make it a surprise."

"No, I didn't ask. I just know it's a girl. Gut instinct."

"You going to be okay with a girl?"

"I'll be more than okay. A little you to love. I'm down with that." He smiled and took her hands in his.

Joanna swallowed a lump forming in her throat. "I know this sounds stupid, but on our second date, I knew I was going to have your children."

Tony grinned. "I thought the same."

"You did?"

"Yeah, on our first date."

They woke in the morning to the sound of knocking on the door. Tony's pulse quickened, and he jumped out of bed and grabbed his gun. No peephole, so he called out, "Yeah?"

"It's Gabriella, *Señor*. Domingo thought you and your family might like some *desayuno*. I have a tray, if you like."

Tony placed the gun behind the door and opened it. "*Gracias, Señora*, the food smells delicious." He reached out and took the tray.

"Will you be leaving after breakfast?"

"No, I think we'll be here at least one more day. Is that a problem?"

"Domingo just wanted to know. There is a couple asking for lodging. I will leave you."

Tony closed the door and brought the tray over as Joanna cleared off the table. Gabriella had made them *enchiladas de pollo*, along with a fresh fruit bowl and oatmeal.

Cortez ate quickly, shoveling the food down.

"*Mas despacio*," Joanna warned. "We don't want you to choke."

"I am hurrying so we can go get my father. Did you find him?"

"Not yet, Cortez," said Tony, his heart falling at the disappointed look in his eyes. "We're going to keep looking today, though. Chew your food."

After they finished breakfast, Joanna had Cortez run the tray back to Gabriella. Tony took the computer equipment back out.

"Did you have any epiphanies when you were asleep?" asked Joanna.

"Nothing. I'm going to check the chatter. See if we've made the headlines." A few minutes later, Tony grinned. "They've got an APB out on both of us."

"And you're smiling?" said Joanna.

"They're making us sound very Bonnie and Clyde. I think that's kind of hot." He raised his eyebrows. "We're believed to have been working behind-the-scenes as spies for decades. It says we're armed and considered very dangerous."

"Shit, Tony, they've probably talked to my parents."

"And my mom. I hope her heart can take it. She was diagnosed with a murmur awhile back."

"I didn't know."

"There's a lot we've missed about each other's lives the last few years." Tony studied her face.

"About Elliot. The truth is—." Joanna started.

The door banged open, and Cortez rushed into the cottage. "*Señor* Tony. I saw the lady. The Chinese lady in the photo."

Tony stood up. "Where?"

"Talking with *Señor* Domingo. The man wanted a room, and he got angry when Domingo said there weren't any more."

"Did they leave?"

Cortez nodded vigorously. "*Señor* Domingo told him about another place to stay down the street."

"Good job, Cortez. Listen. Me and Joanna need to leave for a while. I'm going to ask Domingo and Gabriella to take care of you. That sound okay?"

"You're going to go get my father?"

"That's the plan."

Tony and Joanna packed up essentials into Tony's bag, then locked up the cottage and went to explain things to Domingo.

"I must ask Gabriella," said Domingo, "but if she says yes, then I will agree. We will treat your son like one of our own."

Domingo went to speak to Gabriella and came back beaming. "She is happy to have a little helper *en la cocina. Vaya con Dios.*"

"One more thing," said Tony. "Can you point us to somewhere we can rent a car?"

An hour later, after securing a Corolla from Domingo's nephew, who owned the local junkyard that doubled as a used car lot, they headed for a nearby hotel to start their hunt for the Chinese woman and her companion.

"How do you want to play this?" asked Tony as they stood in front of the hotel office.

"Follow my lead, Clyde," she said, pulling open the front door and sashaying inside.

25

"*Señora*, how can I help you?" asked a young man behind the desk.

"We're looking for some friends who just checked in here. One is a Chinese woman."

"Oh, yes, the couple just went to their room. I can call them, if you like."

Joanna raised her hand. "No, please don't. This is a surprise."

"We just need to know their room number," added Tony.

The young man hesitated. "I'm not supposed to give out room numbers. I'm sorry."

"Don't be," said Joanna, peering out the window behind the man. She saw a couple walk into a room on the far side of the hotel pool. That was mostly likely them, she thought. "We don't want you to get in trouble."

The young man looked relieved.

"Did our friends happen to ask about local restaurants? Maybe we could surprise them there?" suggested Tony.

The clerk's eyes lit up. "They had me make reservations at El Ranchito for lunch today at one."

Joanna clapped. "That's great. Thank you so much."

Outside, Tony pointed to a coffee shop across the street where they set up watch in a window seat facing the hotel.

"I'm taking it you also saw the couple walking into that room." Joanna said.

Tony took a sip of his coffee, then raised one eyebrow at Joanna. "You still an ace at picking locks?"

An hour later, the woman identified as Wang and a man emerged through the doors of the hotel and headed east down the main street. Tony and Joanna waited a minute, then headed over to the hotel, slipping by the main office while the clerk talked on the phone.

When they got to the room, Joanna rapped several times and called out, "Room Service." No answer, so she took out her lock pick that she stored in her go bag and soon eased the door open.

Inside the dimly lit room, Joanna took a second to let her eyes adjust. Women's clothing was strewn on one of the beds. She handed Tony a pair of gloves. "I'll check her stuff. You check his?"

Tony nodded, watching as Joanna found a daybook in the woman's suitcase and began taking photos of the calendar pages.

He wasn't having as much luck with the guy. There has to be a computer somewhere, he thought, checking under the bed and mattress and peering up for loose ceiling tiles. Then he decided to head into the bathroom, where he found a man's toiletry bag. He unzipped the case and looked inside. Typical male necessities. Aftershave, a razor, toothbrush. There was a jar of estrogen cream and a bottle of anti-androgen pills, too. He took out his phone and snapped a photo. Then he looked at the name on the bottle. Song Do.

"Hey, Jo. Can you come in here?" He held out the bottle and jar for her to read.

"Estrogen. Maybe she has hormone trouble?"

"I found it in a men's toiletry bag. Along with these pills. Look at the name on the bottle."

Joanna's eyes widened. "Holy shit."

Just then Tony heard someone at the door. He stuffed the bottles back in the toiletry bag and zipped it, then pointed to the shower. They climbed in and pulled the curtain shut.

Tony heard the room door open, then someone pressing keys on a cellphone. Hard to tell if it was a man or a woman speaking in Chinese. At one point, the conversation became animated. Then silence. A few seconds later, another phone call.

"I'll be right there."

When the door swung shut, Tony said, "Our cue." He whipped the curtain back and went to the door to peer out the peephole, then stood to the side and checked through the curtains. "I don't see anyone, so let's make this quick. On three." Tony turned the knob and opened the door, letting Joanna out first and following. They hurried away from the room, then strolled alongside the pool and to the street.

After they settled down at their stakeout spot at the coffee shop with a plate of glazed and powdered donuts, Joanna spoke. "I don't know much Chinese, but it sounded like he was setting up a meet."

"He was," said Tony, taking a bite, the powdered sugar sprinkling across his chest.

"How do you know?"

"I've been studying Chinese."

Joanna pulled out her phone and showed him the woman's calendar. "Can you make sense out of what she wrote?"

Tony looked more closely. "They've got a meet tomorrow. At the tunnel opening."

"That must be what the FBI agent is coming for, but why take Heriberto?"

"Because it's in an out-of-the-way place? Or maybe they're planning a takeover and need to know the lay of the land."

"Well, we finally know who the leader is. The elusive Song Do." Tony typed into his phone. "What's making my head spin is that our boy wants to be a girl." He showed Joanna a page on a transgender website. "That's what you take when you're changing your sex from male to female."

"Being transgender, as far as I understand, is not something that will go over too well in the 14K. I would think they'd kill him, I mean her, for that reason," said Joanna. "And how is she going to pull it off tomorrow? I think her voice is changing."

"Maybe that's why she has Ju Wang going with her? As a spokesperson," suggested Tony.

"Could be." Joanna strummed her fingers on the table. "I think Do wants out. What better way than to change your identity by changing your sex? They'll be looking for a man, not a woman."

"So, the question is, why does Do want out?" said Tony. "And where does Wang fit into all of this?"

"A temporary companion? Maybe she's going to take over where Song leaves off?"

Just then Joanna spotted Song and Wang heading back into the hotel together. Wang had an armful of women's dresses.

"This meeting may be our only chance to catch Song. He's most likely becoming a she afterward and going underground. God, I wish I could call the office and get backup."

"You can't."

"I know. Watching my hubcaps fly around hammered that point home to me. Not sure if you've noticed, but there are two of us and a lot more of them. Maybe Hammerstein can send in some buddies from the NSA or something?"

"Their jurisdiction doesn't cover Mexico. You know that. We can't call them. We have to go in alone."

26

They headed back to Domingo's, where they found Cortez in the kitchen with Gabriella.

"Smells delicious," said Tony, when Cortez held up a perfectly wrapped tamale. He was glad to see that the boy was keeping occupied.

"*Bueno*," cried Gabriella.

"You finished your business?" asked Domingo, walking in.

"Not quite," said Tony. "Would you mind watching him for the night?"

Domingo turned his attention to Gabriella, who readily answered. "We would be glad to!"

"*Gracias*," said Tony. "If we could have a word with Cortez. Then we'll be off again."

Cortez followed them out into the front room. "We think we know where your father is," Tony said. "If all goes well, we'll bring him back here to you tonight. You just keep having fun with Gabriella and Domingo."

The young boy stood up straighter. "I will behave for them. *Vaya con Dios*," he said as they motioned to leave, wishing them a safe trip. Joanna reached out to hug the boy, giving him a quick peck on his head, which made him blush.

"What are you thinking?" asked Joanna as she hurried to keep up with Tony.

"Grab some things from our room, then head to the hotel where Do and Wang are staying and check in."

"You are back," said the clerk from earlier. "Did you speak with your friends?"

"Not yet," said Joanna, putting her fingers to her lips. "We decided to get a room here and surprise them that way."

"You're in luck. We do have a room. And it is near your friends' room."

"Oh, that's perfect. Isn't it, honey?"

Tony smiled. "Do you know if our friends are in their room?"

"I believe they are." The clerk handed them their keys. "The pool is open until ten pm, and we have complimentary breakfast in the morning."

Once inside the air-conditioned room, Tony pulled two chairs to the window. "I just realized something," he said.

"What's that?"

"We've never been on a stakeout together. Funny, when you think how long we've both been in law enforcement."

They sat without talking, watching kids play in the pool. The shrieks and splashing sounds punctuated the quiet room.

"I can hear you thinking, Jo. What is it?" Tony kept his eyes on Do and Wang's door.

"What was it like? Being alone in the jungle and working on a case. I know you had Jesse, but did you get lonely?"

"Is this a trick question?"

"No. I'm curious is all."

Tony sighed. "Jo, you may not want to hear this, but I was lonely. Every day. For you."

"There had to be other women."

"I've been faithful to you. Ever since you cut me out."

"But I thought?"

"No one is you, Jo. I've only ever wanted you. But you could never see that."

"Tony, I'm sorry." She reached out and touched his arm.

Tony interrupted her. "They're heading out. We gotta go."

Tony grabbed his gun and Joanna did the same. He opened the door a crack and waited until Do and Wang were almost to the street before they followed after them.

"Do is dressed in men's clothing," commented Joanna as a black sedan pulled up to the curb and the couple got in. Tony and Joanna ran to their car, and Tony jumped in the driver's seat, roaring the car to life.

They traveled for a good fifteen minutes, heading toward the tunnel opening. After a while, there were no other cars on the road, so Tony hung back, hoping they wouldn't be spotted. When Do and Wang's car turned, Tony kept driving. "Let's park up around this bend and then go in on foot." The rental car bumped along a dirt road until Tony braked and turned off the headlights.

When they got out of the car moments later, they began running by the light of the moon. After a few minutes, they heard voices in the distance and slowed their pace.

Do, Wang and Stewart came into view. Joanna and Tony stopped behind some bushes.

"I don't like to split up, but I think we should be positioned in two different places," Tony whispered. "I'm going to make my way behind that boulder over there."

When Tony left, Joanna focused on what was being said.

"Wang will take over my duties," she heard Do saying. "I will be a silent partner from here on out."

"I've got too much on the line to listen to orders through some mouthpiece," said Stewart.

"Then we'll be notifying your superiors, Mr. Stewart. We'll tell them all about your accomplices at the agency," said Do.

Accomplices? Joanna was stunned. This ran deeper than she imagined.

"How do we know Wang is giving us directions from you? We'll need a quarterly face-to-face."

"That isn't possible," said Do.

"What do you mean? What else is going on here?"

"He just wishes to spend more time on his other business ventures," said Wang. "Now where is your partner for the funds transfer?"

"Cara," called Stewart.

Just as the name Stewart called sunk in, Joanna felt metal at her back. She motioned to turn, but Cara's voice warned her. "Just start walking toward the group, or I'll shoot."

"Why, Cara?" Joanna asked. "Counterfeit drug smuggling? You took an oath. And your father."

Cara didn't answer, instead pushing Joanna forward.

"Where is the travel guide?" demanded Joanna.

Cara snickered. "He's a little beat up, but he'll live—unless we choose to kill him."

"Why did you take him?"

"As a tour guide, and as insurance, in case you and your nosey ex-husband tried to step in."

Joanna's head swam.

"As you've always said, Joanna, I've come into my own." Cara pushed Joanna into the clearing in front of the others. "Look who I found lurking in the bushes."

"If it isn't the rogue agent wanted for treason," said Stewart. "This makes my job easier. No need to go round you up now. Any last words?"

27

Joanna swung around and faced her assistant. "After all I did for you! You wouldn't have gotten into Quantico if it weren't for me."

"Spare me the holier than thou crap, Joanna. I've listened to enough of your and my father's directives to last a lifetime. Like Stewart said, any last words? Maybe for your mother and father? I can deliver the message."

When Joanna lunged at her assistant, Tony took a shot before Cara did. The young woman crumpled to the ground, then all hell broke loose. Stewart ran to Cara as Wang grabbed Joanna by the throat, aiming a gun at her head.

"Come out, Mr. Molinaro, or I'll put a bullet through your wife's head," she called out.

Tony walked out of the bushes; his gun still drawn. "Let go of her, and we'll talk," he said.

"I always enjoy a civilized talk," said Do. "Although, I prefer it over tea." He smiled as Tony came closer. "It is a pleasure to meet my adversary at last."

"Let her go, Do. Then we can talk about another exchange for the rest of the information I have on your operation."

"Once again, you impress me," said Do. "Ju, release your grip on Mrs. Molinaro, so Mr. Molinaro and I can have a civilized conversation."

"I'll lead you to the information, providing you let both Joanna and Heriberto go. Where is he?" asked Tony.

"He's here. Where is my information?"

"In Puerto Vallarta, but I need to take you to it. And I'm not going anywhere until they're safely away from here."

Do looked at his nails, as if contemplating. "Very well. Let her go, Ju. Stewart, get the tour guide."

"I'm not getting anyone," Stewart cried, his gun on Tony. "He killed Cara, and he needs to pay."

"There are plenty of young women for a lecherous man as yourself," Do said, then nodded his head at Wang, who swung around and shot Stewart in the head. His body swayed before falling lifeless to the ground.

"Now, where were we? Oh, yes. Mrs. Molinaro, heads up, as you say in English." He threw her car keys. "Get your Mr. Heriberto out of the trunk and then get out of here."

Joanna looked at Tony.

"Do as he says. Get Heriberto out of here."

Joanna ran to the sedan and put the key in the lock, opening the trunk to find a bound and gagged Heriberto. He jerked, terror in his eyes, until he registered it was her. Pulling the gag out of his mouth, she worked quickly to untie him and help him out.

"Cortez?"

"He's fine," said Joanna.

"They said he was dead."

"He's safe. I'm taking you to him now."

Heriberto glanced over at Tony, questions in his eyes.

"We must hurry," she said. "Tony will be alright."

As they ran, Heriberto stumbled a few times, Joanna steadying him. Finally, they made it to the rental car, and hands shaking, she pulled the keys from under the seat where Tony had left them and turned the car on. She hated to leave Tony, but they weren't going to kill him until they got their information.

When they arrived at Domingo's, the joy on Cortez's face was boundless. He ran to his father, nearly knocking the man over. "*Papá, Papá.*"

A confused Domingo and Gabriella looked on.

"Forgive us," Joanna told them. "It was for the boy's protection. This is Heriberto, and he is Cortez's real father. Heriberto, this is Domingo and his wife, Gabriella. They've been caring for Cortez."

Heriberto approached the couple, reaching out his hands. "*Mucho gusto*, and *muchas gracias.*"

"It was our pleasure to help," said Gabriella. "You look like you could use a good meal. Cortez helped make some fresh tamales."

Heriberto smiled. "I would be honored, but please let me talk to Joanna for a moment." He turned to her. "*Señor* Tony?"

"I'm a trained FBI agent, Heriberto. You just stay here."

"He has waited for you in Puerto Vallarta. I know you will find him."

Joanna hugged him, then ran to the room and grabbed the hard drive and an extra burner phone out of Tony's bag. She punched a number into the phone.

"Rodriguez."

"It's me."

"Joanna, what the hell? You need to turn yourself in."

"I don't have a lot of time. I'm not the mole, and I need your help."

Rodriguez didn't answer at first. "What do you need?"

"You said you have some buddies in the *Policía Federal Ministerial* here in Mexico? I need backup." She filled him in.

Rodriquez sighed. "Let me get my buddy at the PFM on the other line. Give me a minute."

Joanna tapped her foot nervously as she waited. When Rodriguez returned, he said, "They're sending several men to his place in Puerto

Vallarta. They're also closing down the roads, so likely they'll find them that way."

"They're not traveling the roads. They're using underground tunnels."

After thanking him, she stuck her phone in her pocket and headed out in the rental car towards Puerto Vallarta. Pushing the accelerator to the floor, the old Corolla lurched. From what Tony had told her, they often used motorcycles and quads in the tunnels to make good time. She hoped she could beat them to the cabin.

"Excuse me. I need to be seen right away. I'm spotting."

The nurse seated behind the counter in the emergency room looked up at Joanna. "Are you pregnant?"

"Four months. And I'm high risk."

"Go ahead and have a seat. I'll see if we have an OBGYN on duty."

"I need to see someone now! Just give me someone with an MD."

"Please sit down, and I'll get to you as soon as possible."

Joanna felt a contraction and eased herself into a chair. She pulled her phone out of her purse and called Tony. Straight to voicemail. Again.

"Excuse me, Miss. Can I see your insurance card?"

Joanna went to stand up, and a pain shot through her, causing her to double over and scream. The nurse rushed to her side.

"Easy now. It looks like you're having a contraction. Let me get you a wheelchair. The doctor on duty is ready to see you. Do you have someone we can call? Your husband perhaps?"

28

After walking for a while in the tunnels, Do, Wang, and Tony came to three quads. Do instructed Tony to get on one, and they set off, flanking him as they traveled. As they sped through the tunnels, the sound of the quad engines bouncing off the walls, Tony thought of Joanna. Even if she couldn't find backup, he knew she would come back for him.

At one point, they came to an opening. Do shut off his quad, instructing the others to do the same.

"Are we getting out here?" Tony asked.

"Why would we do that, Mr. Molinaro, when the tunnel runs directly to your home?"

Just then a man came down the ladder from above with two gas cans and filled their tanks. Then they were off once again. The closer they got to his cabin; the more agitated Tony became. He hoped they would beat Joanna there so he could deal with these two before she got there.

"Look man, either turn your phone off or answer it."

"I've got it on in case there's an emergency with Joanna."

"Hasn't she been calling you?"

"Yeah, I'm going to call her back, just as soon as we get this asshole. He's got to be coming out any minute."

Tony's phone buzzed again, and he checked the caller ID. "San Diego Union Hospital."

"This is Tony Molinaro."

"Mr. Molinaro, I'm a nurse at San Diego Union Hospital. Your wife is here. She's okay, but the baby is in distress. We thought you should know."

Tony hung up the phone, face pale. "Joanna is in the hospital. They think she might be losing the baby."

His partner let him take the car, and Tony raced through the streets with his heart in his throat, the car's siren sounding.

When he burst into the neonatal ward a few minutes later, the expression on the nurse's face made Tony's heart drop into the pit of his stomach.

"Are you Mr. Molinaro?"

Tony nodded, afraid to speak as he followed her to a room. "Your wife is in here. We gave her a sedative, but she's still very upset."

"Does that mean—" He couldn't finish the sentence.

"Yes, I'm afraid she lost the baby."

"But at her ultrasound appointment last week, the doctor said everything was going really well."

"I'll find the doctor, so she can explain things to you. The bottom line is that there was nothing anyone could have done." The nurse turned and walked away.

Tony braced himself as he pulled back the curtain and entered.

Joanna turned her head to look at him, despair in her eyes. Before he could speak, she spat, "Don't give me one of your excuses, Tony. I don't want to hear about the lowlife you were trying to arrest while I was losing our baby."

Tony approached her and reached out his hand to grasp hers, but she didn't respond.

"You knew how important this was, but you couldn't be bothered to answer the phone."

"I was trying to get to a place where I could call. We can try again, Jo."

Tears covered Joanna's face. "We're out of money, Tony. And I'm out of energy. I can't do this anymore. You, this. Any of it."

"Things will look better, Jo, once you get home. I'll take some time off and take care of you." He tried to kiss her cheek, but she turned away.

Joanna shifted in her seat. She had stopped for a bathroom break a little while ago and wasn't about to stop again. She prayed she could get to the cabin before they did. That would give her the element of surprise.

Her phone buzzed, and she picked it up.

"Your backup is about an hour out," said Rodriguez.

"An hour?"

"Wait for the backup, Joanna. Stop a few miles from the cabin and go in with them."

"Tony is running solo, and I'm not going to let him down. I wouldn't do it to you, Rodriguez, you know that."

"You have enough firepower?"

"My gun is loaded."

"Joanna, I'm sorry I doubted you, and I'm glad you weren't in your car. Make that mean something."

"Copy that," she said, clicking off.

When she got to the unpaved road, Joanna slowed as the Corolla bumped over the uneven surface. Except for the stars and moonlight, it was dark out here. A sudden impact caused Joanna's head to slam back against the seat, and the car stopped. She had hit something big.

Heart pounding in her temples, she got out and went to the front of the car. Lying on the ground awash in light from the headlights was a big deer, its back legs twisted at an unnatural angle. She gasped when she saw him move. He was still alive.

She couldn't leave him to die a slow, painful death. Getting her gun from the car, she stood over the poor creature, then shot the deer in the side of the head. After a few convulsions, the animal stopped moving.

The car didn't look drivable. Turning off the headlights and slamming the car door shut, she set off on foot.

29

Joanna trudged toward the cabin, using her cellphone flashlight sparingly to guide her path. As she walked, she thought about all the times Tony had tried to get in touch with her since they split up. She'd been so angry, but the truth was, it wasn't his fault. Even if he had been with her during the miscarriage, it wouldn't have changed the outcome.

When she got close, she stopped near the passion vine and listened. Quiet. She stole onto the front porch and tried the cabin door. Locked. She'd have to break the window. Looking around for something heavy, she located a rock and smacked it against the glass until it broke. Then she reached in and opened the door, stepping inside.

Nothing looked disturbed. Joanna started toward the wall concealing the tunnel entrance, when she heard something walking over the broken glass. She swung around to see Sumner in the doorway, a gun pointed at Joanna.

"Take a seat on the couch while we wait for our friends." She flicked the lights on.

Joanna faced her boss, incredulous. "Why?"

"Such a good agent, Molinaro. But so naïve. Put your gun on the floor and kick it to me, now, or I'll shoot your pretty face off. And then sit your ass down."

Joanna put her gun on the floor and slid it over, then perched on the edge of the couch. "What did you do with Cara? Fill her with lies?"

Sumner grimaced. "Someone had to take the fall. She's fish food."

Rage filled Joanna. "She would have made a great agent." Just then the floor of the cabin rumbled as the sound of vehicles approached from the direction of the tunnel.

"I'd worry about yourself, Molinaro. One move, and I shoot you before you can say goodbye to your husband, again."

As the vehicles in the tunnel came to a halt, the engines shut down. The doorway to the tunnel slid open. Wang stepped inside, followed by Tony and then Do, who aimed a gun at him.

"What the hell is she doing here?" Sumner motioned to Wang. "We had an agreement, Do."

"I'm in charge now," said Wang. Without hesitation, she drew her gun and shot Sumner in the chest, sending her flying backwards. Her body skidded along the floor into the glass.

"I'll do the same to you," said Wang to Joanna. "If you don't give me the intel. Now where is it?"

"You're not going to leave us alive, so why pretend?" said Joanna. She began slowly approaching Wang. "You expect us to believe you're going to take the intel and just leave? With all we know?"

"Have your husband get the intel now, or he's going to watch you die a slow and painful death," warned Wang.

"Now that I believe," said Joanna.

"Wang, let us work this out like civilized business people," said Do. "I'm a reasonable man."

"You mean woman," said Joanna. "We know why you're stepping down. We have someone ready to pass that information on to your rival gang if something happens to us. Wang's influence will be nonexistent then. She'll be targeted for sanctioning your sex change."

"You're lying!" cried Wang, waving the gun at Joanna. "Let me shoot her, Do, so her chattering stops."

"Do that, and you'll never get the intel," said Tony.

"Like I said," insisted Do, his voice pitching upward, "we can work this out."

The comment enraged Wang, who swung around to face him. "How are we going to work this out? We were supposed to run things together, and now you're running away from it." She was so upset she didn't notice Joanna inching toward her until she was a few feet away.

Wang swung around, and Joanna grabbed the gun from her grasp, turning it on her and shooting her in the chest. She stood there for a moment with a dazed look on her face and then fell to the floor. That prompted Do to run into the tunnel, and Tony and Joanna followed. When Do jumped on a quad, Tony lunged, tackling him to the dirt floor. As they tussled, Joanna saw Tony try to pin him down, but Do managed to push the gun into his side. She pulled the trigger on her gun, and a shot rang out. Do's head dropped to the floor, a bullet hole in his temple.

Joanna put the gun back in her waistband and reached down to help Tony up. "You okay?" she asked.

"I can get up on my own." Tony struggled to sit up.

"You don't look good, Tony. Your bullet wound is bleeding. I think the stitches came out." Joanna helped him climb the stairs into the cabin.

"I just took down a 14K Triad leader. I should be looking really good right now." Tony looked down and put his hand where blood had begun soaking through his shirt.

Joanna guided him to the couch and went to the kitchen and brought back a towel. She knelt in front of Tony. Pulling his bandage down a little, she checked the wound. "A few stitches just came loose." Now that the adrenaline was ebbing, waves of relief crashed through Joanna. "Thank God you weren't hit. I couldn't lose you, Tony."

Joanna's words hung in the air, then Tony spoke. "I'm right here, where I've always been. Question is, do you want to be right here with me?"

30

"Tony, I never thought I would tell you this. But from the minute you left, I never stopped thinking about you. Almost every hour of the day you were in my mind. The last thing I thought about at night and often in my dreams."

Tony wondered if he had heard her right. "I knew your heart had shattered, Jo. And I just prayed and believed that someday that would heal. All I could hope for is that you would find your way back to me. I have to say, these last years, I had about given up believing that."

"When I lost our child, I felt like such a failure. I could take down the most-wanted criminals, but I couldn't do what other women do every day. When you didn't come that night, my heart just couldn't understand what was happening; how it was out of my control. I'm sorry for refusing to talk to you. It was so very selfish of me. You lost a child, too."

"Oh, Joanna. I had no idea you felt that way." He pulled her to him and held her tightly, her heart beating against his. "All I want, Jo, is for you to say you want to rip those divorce papers into a million shreds...then set fire to them."

"I've never wanted to sign them. That's why they're still in the same drawer I put them in eight months ago when you had me served. And that's why I never served you."

"Oh, Jo, you have no idea how happy that makes me."

When the Mexican authorities finally arrived, they took their statements and hauled the bodies away. Joanna took a moment to call Rodriguez and update him.

"I'm so sorry about this, Joanna," said her partner. "I had a hard time wrapping my head around you being a mole, but the evidence was stacked against you."

"It's okay, I suspected you for a while, too."

"That's understandable, after all my gambling problems. What are you going to do now?"

"I think I'm going to take some time off," said Joanna. "Think things through. Decide what I want to do with the rest of my life. I can't imagine leaving the Bureau, but these last few days have given me a lot to think about." She glanced at Tony, who was talking to one of the Mexican officers and then shut the front door.

"So, you are getting back with your ex."

"We're going to take it one day at a time."

"That's my motto. I'll hold down the fort for you."

By the time the police had cleared out, it was morning. Still too keyed up to sleep, Tony and Joanna went to Heriberto's to check on him and Cortez. They found the two sitting on the Adirondack chairs, eating tamales.

"Glad to see you made it home from Domingo's," Tony commented. "Those tamales look delicious."

"There is plenty for you both." Heriberto motioned to get up from his chair.

"Stay there," said Tony. "You've had a rough couple of days. Joanna and I will get some from the kitchen. Although, later today we could use your help with a dead deer down the way. Joanna told me on the way over here that she hit him last night."

"We already found the deer early this morning when Domingo's cousin drove us home. We have cut up the meat and stored it in the refrigerator." He looked at Joanna. "There is no need to feel badly, *Señora*. You did a good job of putting the animal out of its misery."

Joanna followed Tony to get the tamales. "You've got a swing in your step."

Tony turned and grinned. "Because I have you. No pain. No fatigue."

Joanna smiled. "I'd like some of that."

Tony pulled her into his warm, protective embrace. "I've got plenty for both of us."

The three of them sat together in the clear sunlight, grateful to be home again and safe. Cortez ran over and squeezed in the yellow chair beside his father. Heriberto hugged him and ruffled his son's hair with affection. "Thank you for taking care of my son," he said, "and for saving me."

"If it wasn't for us, you wouldn't have gotten mixed up in all this." Tony reached over and gave the man's shoulder a firm squeeze. "You're a true friend, Heriberto."

"As are you, *Señor* Tony and *Señora* Joanna." The man nodded, then he hesitated. "May I share with you a dream I had last night? Would that be alright?"

"Of course, we would like to hear about it." Joanna sat cross-legged in her chair.

"My wife, she came to me in the early morning. I say it was a dream, but I believe she was there standing beside my bed." Cortez looked up at his father. "I saw in that perhaps half-awake moment, our son under the beloved guava tree, which she planted when she was alive. She watched as he played in its shade." Heriberto hesitated. "But...and this was so real, there was a tiny child running with him, laughing and tumbling in the grass. I have thought about this all morning. My wife, Marlita, she was a very spiritual and intuitive person. I feel as if there is something she wants me to know. Wants you both to know. Time will tell us."

Joanna felt as if her heart stopped for a moment as she and Tony took each other's hands at Heriberto's words.

EPILOGUE

Joanna's and Tony's stories are complete, but Iris's is just beginning...

Joanna's niece, Iris Avena, shut off her computer in the quiet newsroom. On her way out the door, she stopped next to her mentor's empty desk.

Just yesterday, she had sat here with Henry as they reviewed her latest investigative article. Now he and several other colleagues were gone, their desks empty. That afternoon, the publisher had entered the newsroom, and with no explanation, fired everyone but Iris.

"You're the *Recorder's* new head of investigative reporting," the publisher announced. "Congratulations, Iris." Then the man turned and left the newsroom, leaving Iris to face Henry and several other shocked reporters.

Though they avoided eye contact with her as they packed up their desks, their rage and disbelief was palpable. Iris had only been an investigative reporter for a short period of time. The men and women leaving the building escorted by the newspaper's security team had been here for years, some decades.

As they filed out of the newsroom, personal belongings stuffed into boxes, Iris held her breath, expecting them to ask why not her? But no one said anything, which left Iris with a pocketful of questions and no one to ask.

Find out what happens with Iris in *Discovered Denial*...

A NOTE FOR YOU

Dear Reading Gem,

Thanks for spending time with me, Tony, and Joanna! While each of the books in the Discovered Truth Series can be read as a standalone, it's fun to experience the progression and get to know the characters. The series progresses as minor characters introduced in each book become main characters in subsequent books. It's exciting to see what they'll do next!

The Discovered Truth series features complex, gutsy women and equally complicated, charismatic men who find themselves immersed in dangerous and intriguing modern-day challenges, such as human trafficking, drug smuggling, national security threats, and identity theft. When the heroine and hero meet, worlds collide and sparks fly, kindling unforgettable romance and intrigue.

If you like the series, please leave a review on any book review platform. Your opinion matters and is incredibly powerful.

Thanks again and talk soon!

STAY ENLIGHTENED

Dear Reading Gem, thanks for reading! Let's stay in touch.

Join my weekly newsletter Julie's Reading Gems here. You get a free prequel novella to the series for signing up. There are also weekly give-aways and contests to win free books in the series.

You can also find me on my website at https://www.juliebawdendavis.com/fiction/fiction-books/the-discovered-truth-series/, email me at Julie@JulieBawdenDavis.com, and follow me on Amazon.

Escape to Unforgettable Romance and Intrigue...

YOUR OPINION MATTERS

If you liked this book, please leave a review on Amazon, GoodReads, BookBub, or all three. If you don't wish to leave a review or don't have time, please leave a rating. Every star helps!

BOOKS IN THE DISCOVERED TRUTH SERIES

Box Sets

The Discovered Truth Series Box Set Books 1-4

The Discovered Truth Series Box Set Books 5-8

The Discovered Truth Series Box Set Books 9-12

The Discovered Truth Series Box Set Books 13-16

www.ingramcontent.com/pod-product-compliance
Lightning Source LLC
Chambersburg PA
CBHW022026170626
46808CB00003B/1072